THIS 📖

BELONGS TO

All Mary

THIS 📖 IS FOR THE 🦉 MAN BECOS

HE WAS SO KIND 🌱🐥 FOR LEAH

BECOS SHE FOUND ME W🐔

I WAS A LOST 🐷

🐱 ✈️

EGMONT
We bring stories to life

First published in Great Britain 1931.
This edition first published in Great Britain 2017 by Egmont UK Limited
The Yellow Building, 1 Nicholas Road, London W11 4AN
www.egmont.co.uk

Text copyright © The Estate of Gwynedd Rae 1931
Illustrations copyright © Clara Vulliamy 2017
Alphabet design © Clara Vulliamy 2017
The moral rights of the illustrator have been asserted.

ISBN 978 1 4052 8123 2

A CIP catalogue record for this title is available from the British Library.

All Mary

A Mary Plain Adventure

GWYNEDD RAE
CLARA VULLIAMY

EGMONT

Contents

Foreword

by Clara Vulliamy, 2017

I have loved Mary Plain since I was very young, and have longed to illustrate her stories ever since I could first properly hold a pencil.

The books were read to me by my mother, the author and illustrator Shirley Hughes, whose own mother read them to her, and I in turn have read them to my children. Iconic Mary-isms have entered our family language. We plan 'svisits' instead of visits, and write notes to each other in Mary picture writing. When uncertain, sad or homesick, we find Mary's wobbly words, 'Do you think the twins are happy without me?', say it better than anything else could.

Gwynedd Rae's creation is an orphan bear cub from the bear pits of Berne Zoo. Mary is both bear-like and child-like, a perfect combination, an enormous personality all wrapped up in a small, pointy-eared, browny-grey furry package. Mary can be wilful, cheeky and impossible, with an unsquashable ego and an insatiable appetite. But she is also funny, irrepressibly optimistic and utterly endearing.

I love the world of the bear pits and Mary's extended family that inhabit it – the grumpy older bears and her twin cousins Little Wool and Marionetta. They fall out and make up, just like all families.

Written between 1930 and 1965, the Mary Plain series has an abundance of delightful vintage details throughout. But the universal appeal of the escapades and hijinks of a small bear cub, at large in the sophisticated world of grown-ups, is timeless.

There has been a Mary-shaped gap in the cast list of classic bears in children's books for far too long. I'm so proud and happy to see the enchanting and entertaining writings of Gwynedd Rae restored, and for Mary to become a wonderful companion for another generation of readers. She doesn't need any help to introduce herself, so, in her own words . . .

'I am Mary Plain, an unusual first-class bear
with a white rosette and a gold medal
with a picture of myself on it.'

The Bear Family Tree

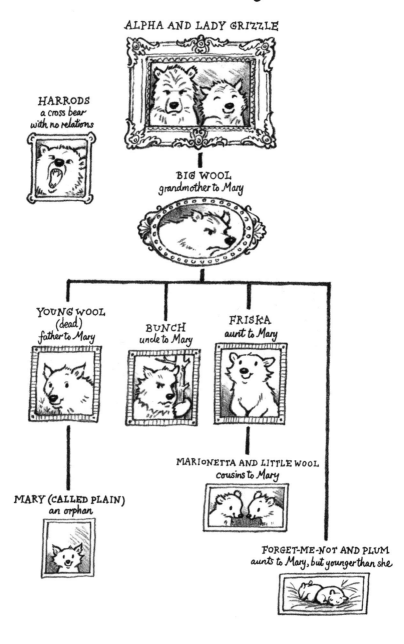

ALPHA AND LADY GRIZZLE

HARRODS
*a cross bear
with no relations*

BIG WOOL
grandmother to Mary

YOUNG WOOL
(dead)
father to Mary

BUNCH
uncle to Mary

FRISKA
aunt to Mary

MARIONETTA AND LITTLE WOOL
cousins to Mary

MARY (CALLED PLAIN)
an orphan

FORGET-ME-NOT AND PLUM
aunts to Mary, but younger than she

. . . and Friends

THE OWL MAN

THE FANCY-COAT-LADY

THE MAGICIAN

SANDY

The Home of the Bears
The Bear Pits, Berne Zoo

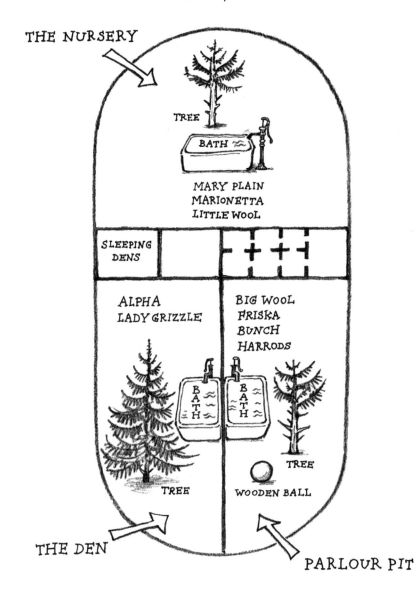

THE NURSERY

TREE

BATH

MARY PLAIN
MARIONETTA
LITTLE WOOL

SLEEPING
DENS

ALPHA
LADY GRIZZLE

BIG WOOL
FRISKA
BUNCH
HARRODS

BATH   BATH

TREE

TREE

WOODEN BALL

THE DEN

PARLOUR PIT

Chapter One

In which things begin to happen

Mary sat on the side of the bath, being important. On her knee was a square blue envelope, and she was stroking it with a paw that shook a little. She had never had a letter before.

Job the keeper had dropped it over the side of the pit a few minutes earlier and called, 'Mary Plain, here's a letter for you.' Just like that!

Mary had played up beautifully. She had strolled across to where the letter lay on the floor of the pit and picked it up. 'Oh, so it is,' she said, and her voice only gave the tiniest shake. Her two cousins danced

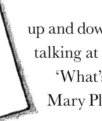

Miss Mary Plain,
The Bear Pits,
Berne Zoo

up and down in front of her, both talking at once.

'What's the writing on it, Mary Plain? Does it say it's for you – and how can you tell?'

'Because it's written on it,' said Mary, who could read her own name quite nicely. 'See, "Miss Mary Plain".'

'Yes, yes,' urged the twins.

'What lives in Nursery Pit,' went on Mary, inventing wildly.

'Aren't you going to open it?' asked Marionetta.

Mary was stroking the envelope and thinking. If there was one thing she hated, it was to admit she could not do a thing, and she knew quite well that she would not be able to read the writing inside.

'I thought perhaps I'd let Friska read it first,' she said slowly; 'it would be such a treat for her.'

The twins stared. Mary was not in the habit of giving Friska treats.

'But it's your letter, not hers,' they said. 'Oh come on, do – *do* – open it.'

Mary gave in, and after a struggle, for her paw seemed too fat to fit under the flap comfortably, she got the envelope open and drew out a big sheet of paper. Mary cleared her throat. 'I'm afraid I can't read it, twins. It isn't my kind of writing at all.'

Just at that moment Friska came out of the den door, so Mary called, 'Please could you come and read this letter for me? It's quite bad writing and I can't understand it.'

Friska at once put on her lesson face and hurried over to the cubs.

'Let me see,' she said. Mary handed her the letter, and she read aloud:

'Dear Mary Plain,
I would be so pleased if you would come and pay me a visit –'

'What's that?' interrupted Mary. 'Is it more than a penny or not so much?'

'A visit is not anything to do with money,' said Friska excitedly, 'it's a stay – a stop – a-a – well – a go-to.'

'Like when I went out to tea, do you mean?' asked Mary, helpfully.

'Yes, but hush, listen to what it says next,' said Friska, her eyes running down the paper. 'Dear, dear, why I can't believe it – I don't –'

'I'm listening,' said Mary. But Friska went on reading the letter to herself, till Mary said again, more angrily, 'I'm still listening and it's *my* letter.'

So Friska read out loud:

> *'I live just outside Berne and I have a lovely big garden where you can play ball and a lake where you can swim, and I think you would be very happy here.*
>
> *I have asked the Owl Man if he would bring you in his car when he comes tomorrow, so have your luggage and yourself ready at three. We shall have such fun.*
>
> *With love,*
>
> *from the Lady in the Fancy Coat.'*

If bears could go pale, Mary would have gone. Instead she took a deep breath. 'Tomorrow,' she said, 'that's next to today, isn't it?'

Friska nodded. She and her twins were all staring at Mary. The twins had that 'not liking Mary very much' feeling that they had had when Mary was asked out to tea and they weren't.

'And what is luggage?' asked Mary next.

'Oh, luggage,' said Friska vaguely, 'well – just luggage. You know.'

'But I don't,' said Mary.

'Well, I haven't time to explain just now,' said Friska hurriedly. 'Now, how do you spell visit?'

However, Mary was far beyond spelling that morning, so she said, coaxingly, 'You'll have to tell me the first time, Auntie, then I'll know.'

'V-I-S-I-T,' spelt Friska, 'and when it's more than one visit, what would it be?'

Mary didn't know.

'Yes, come, come, you know as well as I do. What do you add on?'

'S,' said Little Wool.

'Good boy. Well, Mary?'

'Svisit,' said Mary brightly.

Friska groaned. 'Mary, Mary, you know as well as

I do that's wrong. Think of a word you know – pit. Now what is it with an S added on?'

'Spit,' said Mary.

'Oh, Mary Plain,' cried the twins in shocked voices, 'what do you mean?'

'This,' said Mary, and spat.

Friska gave an angry growl, and was just stepping forward to speak sternly to Mary when she heard the chains rattle, and she had only just time to get back into Parlour Pit before the doors came down. And then Mary suddenly saw a familiar hat up above, and there was the Owl Man.

'Good morning, Mary,' he called down.

Mary waved with both arms. 'I'm going on a svisit,' she said, 'and it's a stay, and a go-to, too. And I'm very pleased, and so are the twins, only not quite so pleased as I am, are you, Twins?'

'Well, it isn't our visit, you see,' said Little Wool sadly.

'Nor our stop, neither,' added Marionetta.

They both looked so dreary that Mary's heart felt sorry for them.

'Just go into that corner for a moment,' she said, 'both of you. I want to ask the Owl Man a private ask.'

The twins looked quite suspicious but went. Mary looked up at the Owl Man and said:

'What's luggage?'

'Well, it means things you bring with you on a visit.'

'Hurrah! Then the twins are my luggage,' said Mary, clapping her paws.

'Oh, but,' said the Owl Man hastily, 'not that kind of thing, I meant things you need.'

'But I need the twins,' said Mary.

'But they haven't been invited. You see, the kind of things I meant were your bowl and your brush. Bears aren't things – they're bears. And you can't take bears on a visit unless they're invited, and the Fancy-Coat-Lady hasn't invited the twins. She hasn't room for them.'

'They could squeeze up quite small,' said Mary wistfully.

'Now, look here, Mary, we must get this straight. The twins are delightful but they are not you, and they are not special friends of the Fancy-Coat-Lady.'

'Am I, then?' asked Mary.

'A very special friend indeed,' said the Owl Man.

Mary was impressed. She backed with dignity to the bath and sat down quite straight and stiff with her arms folded.

'I tell you what, though,' said the Owl Man, 'when I come and collect you tomorrow, I'll bring a box full of surprises for the twins. Cakes, and sugar and figs, for you to give them when you go away. How will that be?'

'Lovely,' said Mary happily.

'And look here, Mary. It's a great compliment to be asked to stay with the Fancy-Coat-Lady, and you'll have to be on your best behaviour, you know.'

'Am I on it now?' inquired Mary.

'Yes, I should think you are.'

Mary got up, looked behind her, and found she was sitting on her letter. She settled herself carefully on it again.

'I'll try not to forget,' she said.

'That's right. Now I must be off, but you'll be ready at three tomorrow, won't you? And I won't forget – you know what,' and he winked at Mary knowingly.

Mary winked back gravely.

'I suppose I couldn't stop being a bear and be a thing instead?' asked Little Wool, who had a hopeful nature.

Mary shook her head. 'I'm afraid not. I heard Big Wool say the other day, "Once a bear, always a bear".'

The twins looked quite disappointed, but on the whole they were really very good about it, and whenever Mary felt specially sorry for them she remembered the basket, and that made her happy again. After all, she thought, you couldn't always tell what a svisit would be like – especially when you had never been on one before. But a basket with sugar and cakes! Well! It was a basket with sugar and cakes!

Chapter Two

In which Mary goes svisiting

It took a long time for the next day to come, at least Mary thought so. She had a very restless night, and wriggled so much that the poor twins got little sleep.

'Oh, Mary Plain, can't you keep quiet?' groaned Little Wool.

'You'll be sorry when I'm gone,' said Mary.

Little Wool knew this was true, so next time Mary kicked him, he just put up with it. At last it was daylight, and Friska came in to tell them it was time to get up.

'Now, Mary,' said Friska fussily, 'Big Wool wants

to see you for a minute, but first you must get nice and tidy. Mr Job said he would give you a good brushing, but he wants me to see to your ears and face,' she finished importantly. 'Are your ears clean?'

Mary bent her head down obediently, but she moved her ears up and down very quickly, so Friska couldn't possibly see.

'Keep still, can't you, Mary?' she said.

'I'm not moving,' answered Mary.

'No, but your ears are,' said Friska.

'I'm sorry – perhaps they're a bit excited today,' said Mary.

'Perhaps you are, you mean,' said her exasperated aunt, giving it up as a bad job. 'Now, come along and say goodbye to your grandmother. She wishes to say a few parting words.'

Mary's heart sank as she trotted off to Parlour Pit. There was nothing Big Wool liked better than making speeches and they were always so dull.

'Well, Mary,' said Big Wool kindly, 'I hear you are going on a visit. Now, remember, you must be on your best behaviour all the time, my child.'

'The Owl Man told me,' said Mary.

'Oh, he did, did he? Well, I hope you will not forget. And you must be very polite. Always shake hands with your right paw – which is your right paw, Mary?'

'The one that isn't my left,' said Mary cleverly.

'And don't forget to say "please", and "thank you" and "how do you do",' continued Big Wool.

'But what do I say if they don't?' asked Mary.

'Don't what?'

'Do.'

'That, I am afraid,' said Big Wool, with dignity, 'must depend. But in any case I trust that you will do us credit.'

'I'd try, if I knew what it was.'

'What what was?' asked Big Wool.

'Credit.'

Really, how Mary did catch one out! 'Well, it's a little difficult to explain,' said Big Wool, 'so never mind.'

'I won't,' said Mary.

'Won't what?'

'Mind.'

Altogether the conversation was not getting on very well, so Big Wool gave Mary a pat on the head.

'Well, run along now, and don't forget what I have told you.'

'No, I won't,' promised Mary, as she went off to the nursery.

Friska had polished her bowl till it shone, and Job gave her a thorough brushing, and then he made a beautiful paper parcel of the bowl and brush, and tied a  label on it with *Miss Mary Plain* written on it.

Inside the parcel Mary tucked her precious letter.

'Now,' said Job, 'just you keep still for once and don't go and ruffle your coat, or the gentleman won't take you along when he comes. He won't want any untidy bears in his car, I'll be bound.'

This sounded very alarming, so Mary sat all the morning on the side of the bath with her parcel beside her and found it the longest morning she had ever spent.

The twins did not have a very good time either. Because whenever they began to enjoy themselves Mary, from the bath, would say, 'You'll be sorry when I'm gone.' And that, of course, ended the fun.

At long last three o'clock came, and with it the Owl Man. He leaned over the wall and called, 'Hello, Mary, are you ready?'

Mary jumped up. 'Oh,' she said, 'I've been here so long keeping smooth for you that it's nearly tomorrow.'

The Owl Man laughed.

'Well, let's get off at once,' he said. 'I'll call Job and he'll bring you up – and this down.' And he held up a big basket all bulging with surprises. Mary was delighted, and went and stood close to the door with her luggage in her paw. Then she heard the key rattle in the lock, the door flew open, and there was Job, with the basket in his arms.

'Twins,' called Mary, 'here is a huge treat for you. It's instead of my svisit.' The twins came rushing up, their eyes sparkling with excitement.

'For us, Mary Plain? Where does it say it's for us?' asked Little Wool.

There were a few odd marks painted on the basket, so Mary, who was very good at inventing, pointed at them and said, 'Here, do you see? It says, "For two left-behind bears!"'

They were both so excited that they quite forgot to say goodbye to Mary, so she gave a little cough and said, 'I'm going now.'

'Are you? Goodbye!' said Marionetta in a cheerful voice, still walking round and round the basket.

'You'll be sorry when I'm gone,' said Mary reprovingly. But the twins did not hear, so Mary went.

Job put on her collar and lead: he said bears never left their pits without them. The Owl Man met them at the top of the stairs and led Mary to a big red car which was standing in the road.

'Is this a tram?' asked Mary.

'No, it's called a car,' explained the Owl Man, as he helped her into the front seat and put her parcel in behind.

'Are you looking forward to your visit?' he asked, as he got in beside her.

'Not just now,' said Mary anxiously, 'I'm looking backwards at my luggage. I'm so afraid the label will blow off, and then we shan't know it's mine, shall we?'

'Would you rather have it in the front?' said the Owl Man.

'Oh, please!' said Mary, so he lifted it over and put it by her feet, and Mary kept touching it with her toe to see if it was still there.

The Owl Man pressed a button, and the car gave a soft growling noise.

'Is it angry?' asked Mary nervously. 'Doesn't it like me being inside?'

'Oh, yes, it's very friendly with bears,' said the Owl Man. 'That's just the noise it makes when it's going to move. Now, we're off!' And sure enough they were.

Another button made a loud hoot when the Owl Man pressed it, and Mary jumped. 'Was that us?' she asked. And the Owl Man said yes, and she could do it next time.

When the next time came and the Owl Man said 'Now!' Mary bent forward, but she was not expecting the corner, and in a second she had shot down the seat and bumped into the Owl Man.

'I'm sorry,' she said, 'but it's a very slidy seat.'

'I know,' he said, and, pulling up at the side of the road, he lifted Mary on to a cushion and tucked a rug round her. 'There' he said, 'now you'll stay put.'

Mary kept a sharp look-out to see if any of the cars they passed had bears in them, but none had. She asked the Owl Man about it, and he said, 'No, as a matter of fact, Mary Plain, you're a very unusual kind of bear,' and Mary felt as proud as proud.

The drive was very exciting, up hills and down hills, and then along straight roads, so fast that the wind blew Mary's pointed ears up on end.

'Doesn't the wind taste nice,' she said, 'all cold and prickly!'

Once, on an empty road, the Owl Man let her help to steer the wheel.

At last the car began to go slower and slower, and soon they turned in at a gate, and after a little bit they came to a white house with green shutters. Mary looked at the shutters hard – she was not very fond of green things. As they drew up by the front door, out came the Fancy-Coat-Lady, and she was all smiling as she helped Mary out.

'Is it because of me you're smiling?' said Mary.

'Indeed it is. I'm so very glad you've come,' she said, 'and I hope you are too?'

'Oh, yes,' said Mary, 'and we've come a long, long way, and I blew the wheel and steered the horn, and the Owl Man says I'm an unusual kind of bear.'

'You most certainly are,' said the Fancy-Coat-Lady, laughing. 'Now, let's go in.'

'Oh, my luggage, my luggage!' cried Mary. 'I must have my luggage!'

'All right, all right,' said the Owl Man, as he got it out, 'I believe you must have some diamonds tucked away in that precious parcel. Here, wait a second while I gather my things.'

'I expect you'd like to wash your paws and then have some tea?' said the Fancy-Coat-Lady.

'I don't want to wash my paws, but I'd like some tea, please,' said Mary, who was always frank. 'I'm very empty down here.' She patted the empty part. 'Please, could I have a carrot or a biscuit?'

'You shall have as many and as much as you want, and now, at once,' said the Fancy-Coat-Lady.

'I think I'm going to like this svisit,' said Mary, as she followed her friend into the dining room.

There were quite a lot of people there. Mary felt quite shy. She clung to the Owl Man's hand, till the Fancy-Coat-Lady said, 'Will you come and sit here by me?' And then she had to let go of it. But when she saw him go down to the other end of the table she ran after him and said, 'Please, I want to sit next to the Fancy-Coat-Lady, but couldn't I sit next to you too? There's room on both sides of me.'

'You bet!' said the Owl Man, and followed her back up the room.

Mary had left her parcel beside her chair, but when she got back she found it gone.

'My luggage – my luggage –' she began.

'Look here, Mary,' said the Owl Man, 'you can't have luggage at the table, you know, it's not what people do. It's there, safe in the corner, and after tea you can have it.'

But it just wasn't any good arguing. Mary hurried off into the corner and began wrestling with the string. The Owl Man followed her, 'Look here, Mary Plain,' he began, 'what about that best behaviour?'

'That's just it,' said Mary, looking quite frantic, 'that's just it! Oh, do, do, open this string for me, please!'

The Owl Man saw there would be no peace till she got her way, so he cut the string. In a moment Mary had opened the parcel, got out her letter, and carrying it back to the table, she spread it carefully on her chair and then sat on it, beaming. Everyone looked very surprised. 'Whatever is that you are sitting on?' asked the Fancy-Coat-Lady.

'My best behaviour, of course,' said Mary. 'The Owl Man said I must always be on it here. That's why I had to unpack at once.'

'You absurd cub,' said the Owl Man, patting her on the head, 'and now, for heaven's sake, get on with your tea!'

'I will,' said Mary – and she did.

Chapter Three

Going to bed in a Mary way

After tea the Fancy-Coat-Lady suggested that it might be a good thing to sit down quietly for a bit.

'Well, if you don't mind,' said Mary, 'I think I'd better run about, I feel quite full.'

'Very well, then,' said the Fancy-Coat-Lady, 'Sandy will take you out and show you the garden.'

'And who is Sandy?' asked Mary.

'Sandy is my nephew,' she answered.

'This is him.' And she put her hand on the head of the small boy, who had come up beside them and was staring at Mary, who still held her letter clutched in her hand.

'Don't you think you'd better let me have that letter?' asked her friend. 'It will be a nuisance while you're playing, won't it?'

Mary looked worried. 'But I promised I'd always be on my best behaviour you see,' she said.

'But supposing you behaved nicely, that would do just as well,' said the Fancy-Coat-Lady. Mary looked relieved and handed over the letter. 'It *is* getting quite rumpled,' she said.

She and Sandy started off together. The garden was lovely. A big lawn with trees growing out of it came first.

'I have a tree where I live,' said Mary grandly.

'Have you?' said Sandy. 'Do you ever climb it?'

'Oh, yes,' said Mary, 'when I feel climby.'

'Do you feel climby now?' asked Sandy.

'Yes,' said Mary. 'Let's race; you up that side and me up this. One, two, three, go!' But it was not much of a race, because before Sandy had hoisted himself onto the bottom branch, Mary was at the top.

'Hello!' she called down. 'Why are you so slow?'

He looked so helpless that Mary came hurrying down to give him a helping paw. They both got pretty high up, and then Sandy said he felt swimmy and he would prefer to get down.

'How can you feel swimmy when you're not in the water?' asked Mary. But Sandy only knew that he did. Mary bundled down first, and because she was very happy and very full of tea, she decided to give Sandy a treat and play the game she and the twins always played when they were happy, so she waited till Sandy was on the branch next to the bottom, and then she nibbled his leg.

'Ow! ow!' yelled Sandy. 'What are you doing? Go away!'

'Only being friendly,' said Mary in an offended voice; 'don't you *like* having your leg bitten?'

'No, I do *not*,' said Sandy, looking very cross.

'And I'm not at all sure I like biting it either,' said Mary, 'it's so pink and bare. Why haven't you got hair on it, like mine?'

'Because boys don't, and it's rude to make personal remarks,' said Sandy. 'Let's go down to the lake.'

Mary stood on the edge and stared. She was just going to say, 'What a huge bath!' when Sandy said, 'That's the lake.'

'I have a lake at home too,' said Mary, not to be outdone.

'Have you got a boat on yours?' asked Sandy.

Mary had no idea what a boat was, so she said, 'Pardon?'

'Have you got a boat on yours, I said?' repeated Sandy.

'No,' she said, 'I haven't – but it's only because I don't want one,' she added.

Next, Mary was introduced to the see-saw, and here she had to give up competing. 'I suppose you've got one of these too?' said Sandy. And Mary, flying up on her end, shouted, 'No, but oh, I only wish I had!'

'What kind of a tree is that?' she asked, pointing above.

'That's a yew tree,' said Sandy.

Mary walked slowly up to the Fancy-Coat-Lady, who was sitting on the terrace with the others. She

pointed to the tree and said, 'Sandy says that's a me tree – a Mary tree.' The Fancy-Coat-Lady looked at Sandy and raised her eyebrows.

'I told her it was a yew tree,' he explained.

'Fancy that,' said the Fancy-Coat-Lady, 'and do you know, Mary, that the tree over in the corner is called a plane tree, so I have two trees in my garden named after you; isn't that a funny thing? And now I am afraid it's yours and Sandy's bedtime. Say goodnight, and I will show you your room.'

Mary looked very sad, so the Fancy-Coat-Lady said, 'Remember, the quicker you get through the night the sooner tomorrow will come.' Mary had not thought of that, so she cheered up and said goodnight all round, and followed her friend into the house. They went into a big empty room, and at once Mary fell flat on her back.

'I didn't know ice was brown,' she said, as she picked herself up.

'Poor Mary! Bad luck! It's not ice really, but it's nearly as slippery, and you must walk very carefully.' With great care Mary got across the room with only one more tumble, and then they went upstairs and along a passage to a room at the end. It had a big window looking onto the garden and, against the wall, a very large bed with a roof on it, held up by four pillars. On the bed was a huge rug. In the corner was Mary's bowl and on a table her brush. Mary walked over to the window and leant out, and there was the terrace just below.

'Hello,' she called. 'Just look at me up here!' The Owl Man called back, 'Pity there's not a green plank, eh, Mary?' And he and Mary had a secret laugh together.

'Well now, Mary,' said the Fancy-Coat-Lady, 'I hope you'll be very comfortable and get to sleep quickly,' and she patted her on the head. 'Goodnight – sleep tight!'

As soon as she had gone Mary began to look round. She looked hopefully at her bowl, but that was empty. Then she tried to brush her coat, but she could only reach the front of herself, so that wasn't much good. Walking about she came to a door she hadn't noticed before, and when she opened it there was a small room, all white, with a big white bowl in it, bigger than Mary. Her eyes fell on two bright silver things at the end of the bowl, and she walked over to have a look at them. Why, they were taps! – like the one in the den at home. Mary turned one on, and out came some

water which made a hissing noise, and the whole room became full of cloud.

'How funny!' she thought, 'I wonder if it's wet water or not?' and she bent over to see.

'OW!' yelled Mary, shaking her paw; then like a flash she was out of the room and tearing down the stairs. She was in such a hurry that she forgot all about the brown room, so she crossed that on her back, and then scrambled out of the window and rushed onto the terrace. 'Oh! Oh! the water's bitten me, the water's bitten me!' she cried, hugging her hurt paw. The Owl Man sprang to his feet.

'Hot water!' he said. 'She must have turned on the tap in the bathroom.'

'Oh dear!' said the Fancy-Coat-Lady, 'I forgot to lock the door. Poor dear Mary!' And she took Mary away and wrapped her paw in a soft white cotton bandage, and it soon began to feel better. Once again they went back to the bedroom and the Fancy-Coat-Lady saw Mary comfortably settled on the bed.

As soon as the door closed Mary got up. What to do now? She wandered round and found near the window a wide flat kind of string just asking to be pulled, so Mary pulled, and there was a loud clatter and suddenly the room was nearly dark. Mary did not like that much and tried to pull it up again, but she only had one paw and could not manage it. She felt her way to the bed and then began wondering what was on top. The only way to find out was to go up and see. With her three good paws she got up one of the pillars quite easily, and she had just hoisted herself onto the roof when the door opened and there was the Fancy-Coat-Lady. Mary lay flat on her face and looked at her over the edge. 'You don't know where I am, so there!' she called.

'I do not,' said the Fancy-Coat-Lady. 'I can hardly see a thing. Why is it so dark in here?'

'Perhaps it's night,' suggested Mary, with an eye on the window.

'Perhaps it's this blind,' said the Fancy-Coat-Lady, and she pulled it up. She looked round. 'Wherever are you, Mary? In bed?'

'No, on bed,' said Mary, from the top.

'Mary, Mary,' said the Fancy-Coat-Lady, 'that's not at all good – what about that best behaviour?'

'Is it naughty to be on the bed instead of in it?' asked Mary.

'Yes, it is at this time. You ought to be in bed and sound asleep. Now, come down at once. I can't think how you got up there with a bandaged paw.'

'With the other three,' said Mary, sliding down the pole.

'I hoped I would find you fast asleep,' said the Fancy-Coat-Lady.

'But you didn't,' said Mary.

'No, I didn't, but now, Mary, you really must settle down. Shut your eyes, and count to ten –'

'But I can't,' said Mary.

'How much can you count?'

'Five every day and seven on extra clever days,' said Mary.

'Well, that's something,' said the Fancy-Coat-Lady. 'You count up to five and then go back to one and do it again and you'll see, before you can say "Jack Robinson", you'll be asleep.' And with a wave of the hand the Fancy-Coat-Lady went away.

'One, two, three, Jack Robinson,' said Mary

quickly, and then waited. Nothing happened. 'Jack Robinson,' she said again, but she was still awake, so she gave up trying and got up again.

She opened the door a crack and a lovely dinnery smell came pushing in. She sniffed it and then began to follow it down the passage. It pulled her all the way downstairs and into the room where they had tea, and there were all the people sitting round the table, eating. Mary stood in the doorway.

'*I* haven't had any supper,' she said.

Everybody jumped. The Fancy-Coat-Lady looked helplessly at the Owl Man, but he had his face buried in his napkin and his shoulders were shaking.

'But surely you couldn't be hungry, Mary?' she said.

'But I am,' said Mary.

'You had such a very big tea,' went on the Fancy-Coat-Lady, 'and you're really far too small to be sitting up to dinner.'

'I wouldn't mind about the sitting, as long as I had the dinner,' said Mary, willing to please. And at that the Owl Man said, 'It's no good, Jill – she wins,' and he pulled up a chair for Mary. So Mary wore a

napkin and ate some soup and custard, and then the
Fancy-Coat-Lady said she simply must not stay up
another moment.

'I can take myself upstairs,' said Mary, 'and thank
you for the dinner,' and off she went. She went up
to her room, and rolled up in the rug on the bed,
but it got into lumps, so she kicked it off and lay on
the bed without it. That was chilly and lonely, so
she picked it up again, lay on it, and began to think
about the twins. And as she thought about them,
and how warm they all kept, snuggled up together
at night, she began to miss them very badly. And
the more she thought about them the more unhappy
she got, till at last she could not bear it any longer.

It didn't take long to find the people on the terrace. By this time they were all getting used to seeing Mary appear, and only the Owl Man murmured, 'Again?'

'I've come to say goodbye. I'm going home,' said Mary. 'Please, will you fetch your car and take me home?'

The Owl Man had a good look at her, and then he put his arm round her and said, 'Now, now, Mary, this won't do at all. You can't come on a visit and then behave like this.'

'Do you think the twins are happy without me?' she asked in a wobbly voice.

'I think so,' he said, very kindly, 'you see, they have each other.'

'That's just it,' said Mary, 'I've only got me.'

This was very true. The Owl Man thought hard and then he said, 'Now, look here, Mary Plain, I know you're a sensible little bear, so just make up your mind to make the best of being here tonight. By tomorrow, after a good long sleep, you'll feel quite different, mark my words.' He got up. 'Now, Jill, we're going off to bed, Mary and I, and I'll see to her getting settled, don't you worry. Just a touch of homesickness, I expect,' he added in a low tone.

'I only ate a little supper,' said Mary, 'but it presses here,' and she pointed to her chest.

'I know,' said the Owl Man sympathetically, 'it's a beastly feeling.'

When they got upstairs he went into the room next to Mary's. 'This is where I sleep,' he said, 'and now I'm going to open the door between our rooms, so you won't be able to feel lonely even if you try, and then I'm going to sit by you till you go off to sleep. I know it won't be long, because you're really very tired.' He brought a chair and put it beside her bed. 'That better?'

'Much,' said Mary. The Owl Man rolled up the rug into a nest, and Mary curled into a ball while he sat down close by the bed.

'I wish you were *my* friend,' said Mary.

'But I hoped I was,' said the Owl Man.

Mary shook her head. 'You're Bunch's,' she said.

'But surely I can be yours too?'

Mary shook her head again. 'You can't be two friends,' she said.

She thought hard for a minute. 'I suppose you couldn't be my cousin?'

'I'm afraid not,' said the Owl Man.

'Nor my aunt neither?' asked Mary.

'No, I certainly couldn't be that,' he said.

Mary sighed. 'Well, what could you be? Couldn't you think of something if you tried very hard?'

The Owl Man did.

'I'll tell you what,' he said, 'if I can't be your friend, I don't see any reason why I can't be your pal, do you?'

But Mary was fast asleep.

Chapter Four

In which Mary behaves as a svisitor shouldn't

Mary was awakened next morning by a tickling feeling in her nose that was nearly a sneeze.

She sat up, and first she had a look at her paw. It was mended, so that was all right. Next she slipped off the bed and ran to look out of the window. All the sky was pink and gold and it must be the next day already. She padded across to the door, but when she turned the handle she found it was locked. So she went instead to the other door, which led to the Owl Man's room and was half open. Peeping in, she saw the Owl Man was still in bed, and she crept nearer to have a look at him. How funny and undressed he looked without his owl's eyes! And every time he breathed he made a strange rattling noise in his throat. It would be a pity to wake him, thought Mary, as she tiptoed away.

Her window was wide open, and when she looked out she found that a long round pipe passed just close to the sill on its way down to the ground. It did not take long for Mary to slide down it, and there she was on the terrace.

Looking round, she saw some small houses peeping over a hedge that ran beside the lawn, so she decided to have a look at them and started off towards them. Coming to a small gate she pushed it open and found herself in a square place, with a good many doors round it. Some were big doors and some were little doors, and some were just doors. Before she could decide which to try first, a swishing noise behind her made her turn round quickly: sitting on the little gate she had just come through was a very large bird with long thin legs and curly tail feathers. It was fluffing out its wings, and when it had shaken them well it stretched its head up and Mary saw it had two red beards, one under its beak and the other on top of its head – a strange place to wear a beard.

'Cock-a-doodle-doo!' said the bird loudly.

Mary jumped.

'Very well, thank you,' she said in her politest voice. She was a little unsure about this stranger and she wanted to keep on the right side of him.

'Cock-a-doodle-Dooooo!' repeated the bird.

'Very well, thank you,' said Mary again.

This duet went on a few times more and then Mary got bored. After all she couldn't stand there all day saying 'Very well, thank you,' so she gave a little bow and turned away.

And then another noise started in another direction. It got louder and louder, and suddenly round the corner came a troop of ducks. Now, Mary had never seen ducks before, and as it was early morning, these ducks were wanting their breakfast and were all quacking their hardest. They seemed so hungry, and advanced with their beaks so wide open, that Mary, in a panic, wondered if they wanted her. She backed against the wall and tried to feel brave and hoped they wouldn't notice that her left leg was trembling a little.

'G-G-Good morning,' she said nervously.

The ducks were now in a large circle in front of her, all out-quacking themselves. As Mary spoke, the largest duck stepped forward.

'What are you?' it said, in a quacky voice.

'Only a bear,' said Mary.

'A BEAR!' – and the duck said it in such a way that Mary flattened herself still closer against the wall.

'Aren't bears allowed here, then?' she asked, in a very small voice.

'How should I know?' said the duck rudely. 'I tell you I never heard of a bear before, so how can I say whether you're allowed or not? And why have you got a fur coat on, on this hot day?'

'I haven't,' said Mary, 'it's me.'

All the ducks laughed quacky laughs, and Mary got a little angry.

'I was told', she retorted, 'that it was rude to make personal remarks.' The ducks looked quite uncomfortable, and Mary began to feel braver. After all, she was the biggest.

'I should like to pass, so would you please stand back there?' she said. Not a duck moved. Then Mary had a brilliant idea. She dropped down on all fours, lowered her head, and advanced very slowly on the ducks, making the growliest growls she could. At the first growl the ducks fled, and by the sixth growl not one was left – only a few frightened quacks came echoing back. Mary breathed a sigh of relief.

The cock had fluttered off the gate, and, closing it carefully behind her, Mary walked down a path close to the hedge. Soon she came to an archway leading into another garden, but she was not very interested in it, because she suddenly felt so empty that nothing mattered very much except how soon it would be breakfast time. However, as she came through the arch, what should she see but a carrot stalk sticking up out of the ground. What a funny way to find a carrot! Perhaps this was a different kind and didn't have the orange end that tasted so good. Mary gave it a pull to see, and, sure enough, up came a long orange tip.

… Half an hour passed, and then Mary went back to the house, walking very slowly. She had never felt less like running in her life. She was extremely uncomfortable inside, and she had begun to feel perhaps she ought not to have got up so early, so when she arrived at the house she climbed quickly up the pipe and into her room. Just as she dropped inside the Owl Man came out of his room and said, 'Hello, Mary, what are you doing?' And Mary leant against the sill, yawned, and said, 'Just seeing what a lovely day it is.'

'Isn't it?' said the Owl Man.

'But I feel quite sleepy,' said Mary, 'and I think I'll go back to bed again.'

The Owl Man looked very astonished – but Mary was often surprising, so he said, 'All right, you tuck up again till I've had my bath, and then we'll go down together.'

Down in the dining room Mary was put on a chair and a napkin tied round her neck.

'And what will Mary have first?' asked the Fancy-Coat-Lady.

'Nothing, thank you,' said Mary.

When Mary said, 'Nothing, thank you,' the Owl Man felt her head to see if it was hot, and the Fancy-Coat-Lady took her into the corner and asked her to put out her tongue. Then Mary was brought back to her chair and they tried again.

'No, thank you,' she said. 'You see, I've had one breakfast and I'm really very full.'

'Had one breakfast? I should think she has!' said a voice from the window, and there on the terrace was a very angry gardener.

'Why, Wilhelm,' said

the Fancy-Coat-Lady, 'whatever is the matter?'

'The matter, madam,' said Wilhelm, 'is that young visitor of yours has pretty well cleared my carrot bed – that's what the matter is.'

'Weren't they for me, then?' asked Mary.

The Fancy-Coat-Lady sighed deeply. 'I am so sorry, Wilhelm, that this has happened. You see, our visitor isn't used to visiting, so doesn't quite understand about things.'

'She understood what carrots were,' said Wilhelm bitterly, as he went off shaking his head.

'I shall not understand them again,' said Mary, 'they have given me a pain.'

'I think perhaps it would be better for you to go and sit quietly on the terrace, while we finish breakfast, Mary,' said the Fancy-Coat-Lady; so Mary went. Soon they all came out and joined her.

'How about a picnic this afternoon?' said the Owl Man. 'It's such a heavenly day, and we could all get into two cars.'

'All right,' said the Fancy-Coat-Lady. 'I'll go and sort out the food, and we'll set off at half-past eleven.'

Mary had no idea what a picnic was, but as long as it included food she was sure she would like it – which showed she had recovered from the carrots.

'What an exciting week,' said Sandy, 'because tomorrow is my birthday, and we are having a party and a magician!'

'Is it a kind of cake?' asked Mary.

Sandy burst out laughing. 'No, it's a person who does all kinds of tricks,' he explained. Mary lost all interest at once.

Sandy was still talking about his birthday.

'I have another birthday soon,' announced Mary, 'and I shall be one.'

'Two, you mean,' said Sandy.

'No, one,' said Mary firmly.

'How can Mary have a second birthday and only be one, Aunt Jill?' asked Sandy.

'Because, my boy, bears have two birthdays every year.'

'I wish I was a bear,' sighed Sandy.

Chapter Five

About the 'pic' and how there weren't any 'nics'

When Mary had been brushed, she and Sandy had a good game of ball, and then, when it was nearly time for the cars to come round, Sandy said he must run up and get tidy. Mary was tidy already, so she waited about in the hall till Sandy came down again. He had a green thing hanging over his arm.

'What's that?' asked Mary.

'My swimming costume,' he said.

'When do you wear it?' said Mary.

'When I swim, silly,' said Sandy.

'Does everybody wear them?' said Mary.

'Of course,' said Sandy.

'I – I left mine behind,' said Mary; 'what can I do?'

Sandy whistled. 'Perhaps Aunt Jill has got an extra one; shall I run and see?'

'Oh, do!' begged Mary. So when the Fancy-Coat-Lady came down she brought a beautiful red-and-white-striped swimming costume which she handed to Mary. Mary hung it over her arm and then, as she heard the cars arriving, she ran out to see which was the nicest to go in.

As she was wondering, two large baskets were brought out and placed on the steps, smelling simply delicious, and Mary's mind was made up at once; she would travel with the smell. The Owl Man came and moved the baskets close to his car, so Mary went and stood beside him.

'Coming with me, Mary Plain?' he asked.

'Please,' said Mary.

The Owl Man opened the door at the back. 'In you get, then.'

'But I'm not luggage,' objected Mary.

'Not luggage! What on earth do you mean?'

'Isn't the back only for luggage?' said Mary.

'No not at all,' said the Owl Man, 'it's for bears,'

and he lifted her in, 'and for boys,' and he lifted Sandy in, 'and for baskets,' he finished, placing the two baskets on the floor.

The drive was very like the last one, only it was much bumpier sitting at the back.

Just when she began to wonder if they were ever going to get there, the cars stopped and out they all bundled. They were beside a large lake, and all round it were woods full of birds singing.

'Shall we have lunch at once?' asked Jill, and everyone said, 'Yes' – so they did.

They all sat on the ground and had lovely things to eat. Mary's bowl was full of meat and potatoes, but it did not stay full for long. Mary still felt a little hungry when she had finished, especially when she saw the other people were still eating, so she turned her head away so as not to see, and when she looked back her bowl had been filled up again – this time with biscuits and figs.

'Like to try some ice cream?' asked the Fancy-Coat-Lady, giving her some in a spoon. Mary gasped. 'It's friz me all the way down my inside,' she said.

After lunch Mary behaved very well, and helped pack away all the things. Then she said, 'And now where are the nics?'

'The nics?' said the Fancy-Coat-Lady, surprised.

'Yes, what we're going to pick,' said Mary.

'Oh, you funny bear!' said the Fancy-Coat-Lady, and everyone laughed so much that Mary felt suddenly shy. So she went up to the Owl Man and said, 'Do you think the twins are happy without me?'

'Help!' said the Owl Man, springing to his feet, 'something must be done at once. Come along, Mary Plain, you and I will go and find something else to pick as there don't seem to be any nics about today.' He and Mary went off, and found some funny fluffy-topped things called dandelions, and the Owl Man showed Mary how to blow the fluff off and tell the time.

'When I was a small boy,' he told her, 'I used to find a whole lot of these where I lived.'

'Didn't you be small here, then?' asked Mary.

'No, I lived in a place a long way off, called England.'

'As far as we came in the car?'

'Much, much farther; and you couldn't get all the way there in a car, because you have to cross the sea.'

'The A B C, I suppose,' said Mary.

'No, not that kind of sea. It's like an enormous lake, so big that when you are in the middle you can't see anything but water all around you.'

'And you don't get tired swimming?' inquired Mary.

'Oh, you don't swim. You go in a big boat, big enough to take hundreds of people.' As Mary could only count up to five she had no idea how many a hundred was.

'Could I come, please?' she said.

'Perhaps, some day,' said the Owl Man, 'you never know. Now, how about picking some of these red flowers to make a nice bouquet for the Fancy-Coat-Lady?' Soon they had a lovely big bunch, and Mary took it back to the Fancy-Coat-Lady. She gave her best bow and said, 'Here's a bucket for you, dear Fancy-Coat-Lady,' and the Lady was terribly pleased and so was everyone else.

Several of the party now said they were feeling very sleepy and would like forty winks. It was boring, but it was not a very long rest after all, because Mary and Sandy were both bad resters and their wriggling disturbed the others.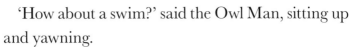

'How about a swim?' said the Owl Man, sitting up and yawning.

'A good idea,' said the Fancy-Coat-Lady, 'we'll go and get ready.' Mary watched carefully to see what the others did, and found they all chose a different tree to undress behind. So she chose quite a nice

pine tree, but Sandy shouted, 'You aren't very private, Mary Plain, I can see you sticking out on this side of the tree.'

Mary moved a bit. 'Is that better?' she asked.

'No, now you're showing on the other side,' he cried.

Mary drew herself up straight

and made herself as tall as she could. She hardly breathed, and felt terribly thin. 'Aren't I private yet?' she called.

'No, you're bulging both sides at once,' was the discouraging answer.

'But why?' wailed Mary, who could do no more.

'Because your tree is too thin. Find a bigger one.'

Mary then ran behind an enormous oak, and this time she was private as private.

The Owl Man set off to the lake. When she heard him, Mary came out from behind her tree. Her arms were through the two legs and the rest of the swimming costume hung in a lump on her chest.

'It doesn't seem to dress me behind at all,' she said anxiously, turning round. The Owl Man bit his lip. 'Look here, old girl,' he said, 'you've got it on the wrong way up – I'll show you. There, that's better.'

'It fits better this way up, doesn't it?' said Mary.

'It's a perfect fit,' said the Owl Man, 'isn't it, Jill?' He turned to the Fancy-Coat-Lady, who had joined them. The Fancy-Coat-Lady looked at Mary and said, 'It's quite the most perfect fit I ever saw.'

Mary proved an excellent swimmer.

'Can I ride on your back?' asked Sandy. He climbed up, and Mary swam out a good way, and then Sandy got quite heavy, so she emptied him into the lake. Luckily the Owl Man was near by, because Sandy could not swim.

'I'm sorry,' said Mary, when Sandy was sitting gurgling and spitting on the Owl Man's shoulders, 'but I thought everyone could swim. And yesterday you said you felt swimmy up in the tree, so, of course, I thought you could.'

'That was altogether a different kind of swimminess,' said Sandy.

When they had all got dressed again, the Fancy-Coat-Lady suggested a game of Oranges and Lemons. Mary's ears perked up, it sounded the kind of game she liked. The Fancy-Coat-Lady and the Owl Man made the arch and all the others marched round, singing. When Mary got her head chopped off and they whispered, 'Oranges or Lemons?' she said 'Both, please.' The Owl Man said she must choose one or the other, so she thought for a moment and then said, 'Oranges, please, and will you please take the skin off, because I don't like its taste.' Altogether a dull game, Mary thought, when they had finished explaining.

Then the Fancy-Coat-Lady looked at her watch, and said if they were going to have tea before they headed home they must begin to make a fire. So everyone went and collected all the bits of wood they could find, and the Owl Man made three long bits of wood stand up on end and hung the kettle of water on them, and soon it began to sing. Mary was very interested.

'Is it happy?' she asked.

'I expect so,' said the Fancy-Coat-Lady. 'Now if you'll tell me as soon as the kettle begins to steam, that means it's ready to make the tea.'

'Yes,' said Mary, who had no idea what steam was. All the same she felt very useful as she stood waiting for it to happen. Nothing did happen for some time, and then some smoke came out.

'There's a cloud come out of its nose,' she said excitedly, 'is that steam?'

'That's right,' said the Fancy-Coat-Lady, and she got up and made the tea, and Mary was very happy indeed, especially about the cream buns.

Then it was time to go back, and they got home quite late, and found a man waiting for them on the doorstep.

'Why, Bill,' said the Fancy-Coat-Lady, 'wherever did you turn up from?'

'I've been here since just after you left,' said Bill. 'I'm over for a week and thought I'd run down and see you. Hello, who's your friend?'

'Miss Mary Plain. Mary, this is Mr Bill Smith.'

'How do you don't?' said Mary, who was quite tired after her picnic.

'Bless my soul, but I don't believe I do don't, do I!' said the man, and everybody laughed. Mary laughed too, but only for a little, for she felt very sleepy. She wandered off, and soon she found herself in the room where they had had their breakfast and she began looking about for a snug corner to curl up in and have forty winks. Near the door she found an open place in the wall with two deep shelves in it, and on the bottom shelf was a bag of meringues. It might have been specially prepared for Mary. She climbed in. Then she got a great fright, for suddenly it was quite dark inside, and she was dropping down, down, down. It dropped so fast that only part of Mary seemed to drop too, and then with a bump it stopped. Mary tried to find a door but there was none, so she decided she might as well have her sleep. The only trouble was that the bag of meringues took up quite a lot of the shelf. Soon, however, there was plenty of room. Mary curled up and fell sound asleep beside a very flat paper bag.

Meantime upstairs, someone said, 'Where's Mary?' and no one seemed to know. The Fancy-Coat-Lady began looking in the rooms downstairs, the Owl Man ran up to see if she was in her room, and Sandy ran round the garden calling 'Mary, Mary!'

They all met again on the terrace, quite out of breath, and all of them said, 'Well?' and everyone answered, 'Not a sign of her anywhere.'

'She can't have gone far,' said the Fancy-Coat-Lady,

'what time is it?'

'Half-past seven,' said Bill, looking at his watch.

'And we came in at 6.30,' said the Owl Man with a groan. 'Plenty of time to disappear.'

'Especially when you're Mary,' added the Fancy-Coat-Lady. 'What can we do?'

'How about the lake?' said the Fancy-Coat-Lady. 'She wouldn't go out in the boat alone, by any chance?' So they all rushed down to the lake. But there was the boat and no sign of Mary. Then they all went back to the house, and everyone looked very worried.

The Owl Man looked at his watch. '8.30. I think I'll get the car and drive along the road,' he said. 'She's such an odd little creature – perhaps she said, "I wonder if the twins are happy without me," and there was no one there to answer, and so she started off home. Yes, I'll go and get the car.'

'Wait a minute,' said the Fancy-Coat-Lady. 'I absolutely insist on your having something to eat before you go. It's a cold supper because the cook is out, so it won't take a minute to get it ready. Come along into the dining room.'

The Owl Man followed her in, and the Fancy-Coat-Lady went over to the lift and pulled the rope. 'Bother,' she said, 'this lift's gone wrong again.'

'Let me try,' said the Owl Man. He gave a strong pull and the lift began to move. 'It's coming now,' he said, 'but whatever can there be for supper? It's as heavy as lead.'

'Just cold beef and meringues,' said the Fancy-Coat-Lady.

But it wasn't meringues – it was Mary.

Chapter Six

How Mary did her best to help the magician

Mary slept quite late next morning; in fact the Owl Man had to give her a poke to wake her up.

'How about some breakfast,' he said, 'or do you want more sleep?'

'No,' said Mary, 'I think breakfast would be much nicer than more sleep.' So off they went downstairs.

'By the way,' he said, 'you must be sure to say "Many happy returns of the day" to Sandy when you see him.'

'Why?' said Mary.

'Because it's his birthday,' said the Owl Man.

Sandy was standing near the window when they went in, and Mary went up and said, very nicely, 'Many happy returns of the day, Sandy.'

'Thank you,' said Sandy.

'And are these the returns?' asked Mary, pointing to a table piled with presents.

'Those are all my presents – aren't they lovely?' said Sandy, in an excited voice.

'Perhaps they are, under the paper,' said Mary; 'aren't you going to look?' So Sandy unpacked them and found they were all just the very things he wanted most. Especially the gramophone!

'Now, I really think you must get on with your breakfast, Sandy,' said the Fancy-Coat-Lady. 'You can go back to your presents afterwards. Come along.' So they all sat down at the table.

There was nothing wrong with Mary's appetite this morning, and nobody had to ask her to put her tongue out. When the Fancy-Coat-Lady said, 'What first, Mary?' she said, 'Thank you, I'll start at the beginning and go on to the end.'

'And don't forget the middle,' said the Owl Man.

'I won't,' promised Mary, and kept her word.

'Tell us some more about this business that's

brought you over here, Bill,' said the Owl Man.

'Well, it's to do with this big show at Earl's Court that's to start next week. The idea is to give people who own any odd animals a chance of showing them.'

'What sort of animals?'

'Well, anything you like – from performing fleas to elephants – excluding horses, dogs, and cats. I believe there are a fair number of entries already, among them some tame slugs and a hippo trained to walk the tightrope. Any unusual animal can be exhibited.'

'That's me,' said Mary, 'you said I was unusual, didn't you, Owl Man?'

'I did,' said the Owl Man.

'And you're certainly an animal,' added the Fancy-Coat-Lady.

'I say,' said the man called Bill, and he started talking to the Owl Man in a low voice. As he talked the Owl Man stared at Mary in an odd kind of way. Mary felt quite uncomfortable.

'Have I come unbrushed?' she asked, trying to see her own back.

'No, no, you're all right,' said the Owl Man, but he

still looked so strange that Mary began not to like it at all.

'Do you think the twins are –' she began. The Owl Man stopped looking strange at once. 'I'm quite sure they are, Mary. And now if you've finished your breakfast, I'm sure the Fancy-Coat-Lady wouldn't mind you going out into the garden.'

'Of course not.' So Mary ran on to the lawn and did a bit of jumping, just to keep in practice, and when she had finished the Owl Man called her over to him.

'Do you remember me telling you about my home, Mary Plain?'

'Yes,' said Mary brightly, 'over the B – a long way off.'

'Nearly right! Over the sea. Well, how would you like to go there on a visit?'

'Today?' asked Mary.

'No, not today, but quite soon.' Mary felt a little giddy.

'Do you mean I'd be your svisitor?' she said.

'Yes,' said the Owl Man.

'But won't Bunch be angry?'

'I don't see why he should,' said the Owl Man; 'as a matter of fact he'd be too old to go.'

'I'm nearly one,' said Mary in a grown-up voice.

'Yes, I know, but I think she'd be allowed, don't you, Bill?'

'I do indeed,' said Bill.

'Well, Mary, it's for you to say. You must decide if you'd be happy; no one can tell that but yourself.'

So Mary went into the corner by herself and said, 'Mary Plain, would you be happy to go on another svisit with the Owl Man?' and Mary Plain answered 'Yes, Mary Plain, I would.'

So that settled it.

Then Sandy carried the gramophone out under the trees, and he and Mary played soldiers. There were some lovely marchy tunes, and Sandy taught Mary how to march, and how to stand at the salute when they sang 'God Save the Queen'. Mary even learnt to say 'God Save the Queen' with a strong Swiss accent. Then it was lunchtime, and afterwards Sandy and Mary were sent up to rest for an hour, to be fresh for the party.

'Run up and lie down, Sandy, there's a good boy, and put on a clean white shirt and your new corduroy trousers, because you must look festive for the party,' said the Fancy-Coat-Lady. 'The children are coming at three, so make sure you are ready by then.'

'Must I look fes – what you said – too?' said Mary.

'Yes, of course,' said the Fancy-Coat-Lady.

'Then shall I put on my swimming costume?' said Mary.

'I am afraid it wouldn't be quite suitable,' said the Fancy-Coat-Lady kindly.

'It's all the clothes I've got,' said Mary, her voice quite quaky.

'I tell you what,' said the Fancy-Coat-Lady hastily, 'I've got some lovely wide blue ribbon and you shall wear a big bow of that. How would that be?'

'Where would I wear it?' asked Mary.

'Round your neck. You will look splendid.'

So when Mary came down at three, she wore a beautiful satin bow just behind her left ear, and everyone said she was the smartest bear they had ever seen.

Lots of children came, and they were all most interested in Mary. She had to shake hands so often that her paw began to ache.

'My how-do-you-do paw is tired,' she said to the Owl Man, 'what can I do? Shake hands with my back one?'

'Why not your left?'

'Because Big Wool said it must always be a right one,' said Mary.

'I think a very good bow would do as well,' said the Owl Man resourcefully.

They all played hide-and-seek to begin with, and then had some races. Mary came in third in a three-legged race and won a large red ball, which was very exciting. After that came tea – and such a tea! A huge white-iced cake stood in the middle of the table with seven candles burning on it, and by each plate was a pile of crackers.

Mary did not know about crackers, and when they began to go off she put her paws up over her ears. 'Do you think the twins are –' she began.

The Owl Man was standing behind her and said, 'Don't worry, Mary – just hold tight on to the other end and pull hard, and perhaps you'll get a hat or a present.'

The next minute Mary was wearing a delightful little sailor hat on one side of her head, but though she pulled a few more, she was not really happy till cracker time was over.

Then came the most thrilling part of the whole party. They all went into the big slippery room, and there were lots and lots of chairs, and at the end a platform. And on the platform was a very friendly man dressed in grey. He was called a magician.

'Good evening, young ladies and gentlemen,' he said. 'It is a great pleasure to see so many little people here this evening, and I hope we are going to have a pleasant time together. But, you know, it isn't very easy to have a nice time all by oneself, and as I shall be wanting a little help now and again, I hope some of you will be willing to lend me a hand.'

'I could lend you my paw,' said Mary, but everyone said 'Ssh!'

The magician did a great many wonderful things. He made twelve silk handkerchiefs come out of a ball, and shook them into a flag. He showed them an empty box and then blew on it, and when he opened it again there was a lovely flower growing in it; and then he made a real live rabbit come out of a top hat. Each time he finished a trick, the children clapped,

and he came forward and bowed, and every time he bowed Mary got down off her chair and bowed back.

'Now,' said the man, 'I will do a little mind-reading. I am going to place a blackboard on the platform. Then I am going to ask someone to come and blindfold me with this thick silk handkerchief. I shall then be able to see absolutely nothing. I shall sit on this chair, and then I want one of you young ladies or gentlemen to come up and write a little poem about yourself on the blackboard, and go quietly back to your seat. I will then remove the handkerchief, and when I have read the poem I will tell you who has written it. Now – if someone would be so kind as to fix this scarf? Thank you, sir.

'There, ladies and gentlemen, I cannot see anything at all,' and the man gave a little bow from where he sat.

Mary bowed back, as usual. She felt very sorry for him all wrapped up in the black scarf.

Then the Owl Man crept up onto the stage and wrote: 'I'm small and fat, and I wear no hat,' and crept back to his place. The children were all laughing – they felt sure the magician would never guess. But he did! He walked up to the board, looked at it hard, and then turned and pointed straight at the Owl Man; 'I think that that gentleman wearing glasses has written this,' he said. Everyone clapped very hard because of his cleverness. They blindfolded him again, and then Sandy went up and wrote:

'I'm not a girl, I'm not a man,
So just you guess me if you can.'

And again the magician guessed right. Then a short little girl had a turn, and she had to be lifted up to reach. She wrote:

'If you can guess me,
You'll be clever, d'you see.'

But he did.

Mary was tremendously excited. She ran and pulled the Owl Man's sleeve. 'I want a turn,' she said, 'couldn't I?'

'Of course!' said the Owl Man.

'I've got the poem (Mary pronounced it "pome") but I can't write it,' she explained. So the Owl Man went up with her, and she whispered to him to write:

'I am an unusual bear.
And I don't mind telling you once again,
One of my names is Mary,
and the other's Plain.'

'Is that the right kind of poem?' she whispered anxiously, and 'Yes,' said the Owl Man again.

This time the magician looked very hard at the board before he said, 'Of course it will be extremely difficult for me to guess who this poem is about – *extremely* difficult.'

'Can I help?' asked Mary from her seat.

'That would be very kind.' Mary was helped onto the platform.

'Now, about this first line, "I am an unusual bear." What would that mean?'

'That means a bear,' explained Mary kindly.

'Oh, I see – a bear. That's good. I'm glad you were able to tell me that. And next – "One of my names is Mary"?'

'Yes, that's quite right,' said Mary excitedly, 'the first one *is* Mary.'

'Excellent – we're doing well! And the last line – "And the other's Plain"?'

'It's the second name,' said Mary, jumping up and down, 'and now, can't you guess?' The man looked doubtful and shook his head, and Mary could not bear it any longer.

'It's me,' she shouted, 'it's me! I am Mary and a bear and Plain and it's me.'

There was a roar of clapping and laughter all through the room, and the magician took Mary by the paw and they both bowed and bowed.

The next thing was that the magician held up a gold watch and asked everyone to have a good look at it. Then he put it in a little box on the table and locked it with a key, which he handed to a boy in the front row to keep safe.

'Now, I suppose no one can guess where that

watch will be found?' asked the magician.

'I can,' said Mary unexpectedly.

Everyone turned and looked at her, and the man gave a little laugh and rubbed his hands together. 'Well, well,' he said, 'if this young – er – lady –'

'Bear,' corrected Mary.

'I beg your pardon – if this young bear – Miss?'

'Mary Plain,' said Mary.

'Thank you, if Miss Mary Plain can find that watch she'll be a wonder.'

'I am unusual, you know,' said Mary modestly, 'but I'd like to be a wonder too. May I try?'

'By all means,' said the magician, but you could see from his smile he felt a bit sorry for her.

Mary climbed down from her seat, went straight to the Owl Man, put her paw in his left-hand pocket – and held up the gold watch. 'There,' she said.

There was tremendous clapping and shouting, and Mary had to be helped on to the stage again to do more bowing. And Sandy called, 'However did you guess, you clever Mary Plain?' Mary was just stepping off the platform, but she stopped and said, 'Because I saw the magician put it in the Owl Man's pocket before tea.' Loud and deafening applause followed Mary as she left the platform.

Now Mary did not realize it, but she was tired out. She did not go back to her seat; she wandered behind the platform and had a look round. There were a few things like handkerchiefs and hats lying about, and in the corner a big red-and-white-striped barrel. 'Just like my swimming costume,' thought Mary, and it made her feel very friendly towards the barrel.

Meantime the magician was getting to the end of his programme. He told the children he would now show them his best trick of all – the last and the best.

'Do you believe in fairies?' he asked. All the little girls said 'Yes,' and the little boys tried to look as if they didn't.

'Well,' he said, 'the first thing I am going to show you is an empty barrel,' and he rolled the red and white barrel onto the middle of the stage.

'Now this barrel is empty,' he said, giving it a tap with his magic wand. 'Come in,' said a faint voice. The magician stopped a moment and looked towards the door. Then he continued, 'This barrel is completely empty,' and he walked right round it, tapping as he went. Two or three times he thought he heard 'Come in' again, but he took no notice.

'Now, though I have assured you that there is nothing in this barrel, you would no doubt like me to prove it to you. As the saying goes, "seeing is believing". So I will remove the lid and show you it is full of – emptiness!'

'But it's full of me!' said Mary, popping up through the hole, with a very ruffled head and her pointed ears and blue bow all standing up in an excited kind of way. 'Why did you say it was empty?' she asked indignantly. When Mary appeared the poor magician had sat down quite suddenly, and he looked quite white.

'Because I thought it was – because I was absolutely dead certain it was,' he said in an exhausted voice.

'But I thought magicians could guess everything,' said Mary, 'and you are a magician, aren't you?'

'I'm beginning to doubt it,' said the man.

The great excitement caused by Mary's appearance in the barrel began to die down, and one or two children called out, 'Where's the fairy? We want to see that fairy.' The magician stood up.

'And so you shall, young ladies and gentlemen – if someone would –' he pointed helplessly at Mary, who was still sticking up out of the barrel.

'Certainly,' said the Owl Man, and, jumping onto the platform and lifting Mary out, he carried her to the back of the room. There, with the Owl Man's arm firmly round her waist and the Fancy-Coat-Lady holding one of her paws tightly, Mary was safe.

And it was a lovely ending to a lovely day. For the magician, after showing them the now really empty barrel, pulled in a box, and stood the barrel on top 'so they could see better'. Then he tapped on it with his wand and cried 'Abracadabra!', and out came a lovely little fairy with blue eyes and curly hair. In her arms she held a basket made of silver, and in the basket were lots of coloured paper parcels. These she threw among the children, and they caught them and inside each parcel was – well, just you guess!

Chapter Seven

In which Mary sends out some invitations

The day after Sandy's birthday the Owl Man had to go away, and as Mary was to go to England with him so soon, it was decided that he should take her back with him to Berne.

'But I'm sure the twins are happy without me, and I'd rather stay here, thank you,' said Mary when she was told. 'You see, I'm liking this svisit so much,' she said.

'But you'll be going on another next week,' said the Owl Man encouragingly.

'It might not be as nice,' said Mary, sighing.

The Owl Man sighed too. It was sometimes a little difficult to please Mary. Several times during her stay she had wanted to go and see if the twins were happy, and now that she had a chance of going, she was determined to stay.

The Fancy-Coat-Lady tried to help. 'You'll come again some day soon, I hope, Mary, and you have got a lot of things to tell the twins about, haven't you?' Mary brightened; she hadn't thought of that.

'And I tell you what,' said her friend, 'how would you like to take back a big box of cakes and biscuits and things, and then give a "welcome home" party to all the bears?'

Mary's eyes shone. 'Would it be my own party?' she said.

'Of course, your very own. You would have to send out the invitations and sit at the head of the table, like I do here.'

So when Mary went off with the Owl Man she was comforted by the thought of the large box on the back seat. She really had quite a lot of luggage. Her bowl and brush and her swimming costume and sailor hat and bow made one quite large parcel. Both that and the box were labelled *Miss Mary Plain*, but the box had *Private* written on it too.

Before she had realized it, there they were back at the pits.

Mary looked round. Everything seemed just the same as when she had gone away all that long time ago. She felt very well-travelled as she got out of the car and shook hands with Job, who had come forward to meet them.

'Hello,' he said, 'where's your collar? Lost it?'

'No, here it is,' said the Owl Man, 'but she hasn't worn it since she left as there seemed no need. She has been very good on the whole.'

'Which whole?' inquired Mary. Both men laughed.

'Isn't she a character?' said Job. 'I must say we've missed her here.'

'Well, you'll be missing her more soon,' said the Owl Man, 'because I'm taking her over to England next week; I've come up today to make all the necessary arrangements,' and he told Job all about the show.

While they talked, Mary ran across to look through the railings into Parlour Pit.

Harrods was lying in the corner asleep, as usual, Bunch sat on his branch, and Friska was over on the other side of the pit playing with an empty milk bottle.

And Big Wool? Well, Big Wool was just under Mary, doing her best trick. She was lying flat on her back, holding her front paws with her back paws and sticking out her tongue as far as it would go. Though very charming, it was not a dignified position to be found in by your granddaughter, and directly Big Wool saw Mary she lumbered to her feet and hoped she had not noticed her.

'What are you lying on your back like that for?' asked Mary. Big Wool pretended not to hear. She gave herself a shake, looked up, saw Mary, and said. 'Well, well,' she said, 'back again, Mary? Fancy that.'

'Yes I am,' said Mary, 'but I want to know what you were lying on your back like that for?'

'Just for a rest,' said Big Wool.

'Is it a rest to hold your toes like that and hang your tongue out such an extra long way?' said Mary.

Big Wool was starting to wish Mary had stayed away before she changed the subject.

'When did you get back?' she asked, and then she called to Friska that Mary was back.
Friska hurried up.

'Good morning, Friska,' called Mary, and, 'good morning, Bunch.' Friska waved her paw, but Bunch took no notice at all; perhaps he was a little jealous at seeing Mary so friendly with the Owl Man.

'So you're all still here,' said Mary, looking down on them.

'Where else could we be?' asked Friska.

'Oh, I only thought someone might have invited you on a svisit as well,' said Mary.

Big Wool, Friska, and Bunch all tried to look as if they wouldn't go on a visit if they were asked, but only Bunch succeeded.

'Now, Mary,' said Job, coming up behind, 'you must go back to your own pit, I can't let you stand about like this or I shall be getting into trouble.' So Mary shouted, 'Goodbye till I see you again,' and went off.

The Owl Man followed her. 'I must be off now, Mary Plain. I've got a lot of things to settle before we go. One day I shall have to take you to the barber's, by the way, and have your coat trimmed.'

'Trimmed with what?' inquired Mary.

'Scissors, of course,' said the Owl Man.

Mary had a vision of herself with scissors sticking out all over her. It seemed a bit odd, but the Owl

Man had said 'of course', so perhaps bears going to England always wore scissors. Anyhow she'd wait and see before she said she'd rather not.

'Meantime, you'll keep her well brushed, won't you, Job?' said the Owl Man, and Job promised he would, and Mary was sorry, because she hated being brushed.

'Well, *au revoir*, Mary. Be good,' said the Owl Man.

'Aren't I always, then?' asked Mary.

'More or less,' said the Owl Man, laughing. 'Now, I really must go.' He gave Mary a final pat on the head and then went over to Parlour Pit and had a few minutes' chat with Bunch about sugar. Then he jumped into his car, waved to Mary, and was off.

Mary turned and peeped through the railings of Nursery Pit, and there were Marionetta and Little Wool. Directly she saw them, Mary realized how much she had missed them. They were playing a climbing game, and Little Wool was balancing in a very unsteady position on a branch which hung over the bath.

'Boo!' said Mary, through the railings. There was a loud splash, and then a second one, as Marionetta joined Little Wool by mistake.

'It's Mary Plain,' shouted Little Wool, as he

clambered spluttering out of the bath. 'She's come back!'

'Yes, I've come back,' said Mary. 'Wasn't it good of me?'

Before the twins could answer, Job pulled Mary away from the railings and said she must really hurry down. On the way Mary told him about the party she wanted to give next day, and Job promised he would keep the things all safely put away till then.

'You look just the same,' said Little Wool, walking slowly round her. 'Visits don't change you at all then?'

'Only inside,' said Mary. 'I've got lots of things inside that you don't know anything about, you see.'

'Carrots?' said Marionetta enviously.

'Carrots!' said Mary. '*And* figs, *and* biscuits, *and* cakes, *and* porridge, *and* potatoes, *and* CREAM BUNS!!!!'

'What are they?' asked Little Wool.

'They are round and you bite them and cream spills into your mouth,' said Mary.

Little Wool licked his lips.

'And did you eat cream buns all the time?' he asked.

'Most of it,' lied Mary, 'and when we weren't eating we were doing very exciting things.'

'Oh, what? Please tell us,' begged the twins. So all three sat down in a shady corner, a twin on each side of Mary, while she told them all about everything she had done, and quite a good deal she hadn't.

'And now you are going away again,' said Little Wool. 'Why couldn't Marionetta and I go instead this time?'

Mary shook her head. 'You see,' she said, in a very confidential voice, 'it's because I'm unusual.'

'What does that mean?' said Little Wool.

'I don't know,' said Mary, 'but I'm it. That's why I'm going away on another svisit.'

The twins sighed. 'Never mind,' said Mary, 'I'll tell you all about it when I get back. And there's to be a party tomorrow.'

'A party?' cried the twins brightening up at once. 'Whose?'

'Mine,' said Mary, 'but it's to be a surprise, and I shan't tell you anything about it till it happens, so don't ask questions.'

'I'll try,' said Marionetta.

'Could I ask just one?' said Little Wool.

'Is it a very big one?' said Mary. Little Wool shook his head.

'Ask,' said Mary.

'Will there be cream buns?' said Little Wool, in a hoarse whisper.

'No, you may not,' said Mary.

'Mayn't what?' said Little Wool.

'Ask one question.'

'But I have, and you said, "Yes".'

'That was a mistake,' said Mary. 'I wasn't thinking. But now I must write the invitations.'

'What are invitations?' said Little Wool.

'Oh, they're "askings", "will you comes", that you send to people before a party. I've got some paper that the Fancy-Coat-Lady gave me; I'll run and get it.'

The paper was spread on the floor, and Mary lay on her front and wrote with a red pencil and an anxious expression. She wrote it in 'Mary writing':

D BIG WOL AND FRIZCCA AND
AND HARUDS.
AM HAVR A PARTIE
II MORO AND THIS IZ AN MISS M. PLAIN AT HOME 2
ASK U ALL 2 KUM 4 AND . IT IS
GOING TO A SPESHALLY LUVLY
PARTIE AND DO HOPE U WILL
TH .
LUV AND X X X X
FROM

The twins were full of admiration over the letter.

'It's a beautiful letter,' said Marionetta.

'It is rather,' acknowledged Mary. 'Now, Mr. Job must take it to them so I can hear whether they can come.'

'Mightn't they be able then?' asked Little Wool.

'You never know,' said Mary.

'Why?' said Little Wool.

'Oh, well,' said Mary, 'Harrods might have broken her leg, or Friska might have caught a chill.'

'What is a chill?' asked Marionetta.

'Don't you *know*?' said Mary, who had no idea herself.

'No,' said Marionetta.

'Then I shan't tell you,' said Mary.

'Do you catch it in your mouth?' asked Little Wool.

'Sometimes, in your swallow,' said Mary.

But none of these alarming things happened. Job delivered the letter. The envelope was addressed like this,

To BIG WUL
To FRIZCCA
To MR BUNSCH
To HARUDS

and its arrival caused great excitement in Parlour Pit.

Big Wool was eldest, but Friska was the best reader, so she read it out loud. Bunch refused to come down from his branch, so the others had to stand underneath, and Friska read in a very loud voice so he could hear. When she had finished Big Wool scratched her head and said, 'Is it proper for a small bear to give a party for us big ones?'

Friska looked very worried . She had been thrilled at the idea of going.

'What do you think, Bunch?' she said looking up at him.

'I don't think,' said Bunch. And that was all they could get out of him.

'So we shall have to decide,' said Friska, looking anxiously at Big Wool. Big Wool thought for a bit, and then she said, 'Perhaps it would be a shame to disappoint the cub.'

'Especially just when she has got back,' said Friska eagerly. She was simply longing to go.

So it was settled that they would all go, and Friska wrote a letter in real bear writing, which, as you know, can only be read upside down.

Dear Mary Plain,

We would all like to come, so we will, thank you,

Big Wool,

Friska,

Bunch,

Harrods.

Friska had to borrow some notepaper from Job, and when the letter was written he took it to Mary.

'What does it say, oh, what does it say?' said the twins, looking over her shoulder. Mary read aloud,

'Dear Miss Mary Plain this letter is from Big Wool and Bunch and Harrods and me to say we will be delighted to say yes to your very very very kind invitation to your party we think you are the kindest bear we have ever heard of and I am proud because you are my niece and Bunch is proud because you are his niece and Big Wool is proud because you are her granddaughter and Harrods would be proud too only she is asleep with heaps and heaps of kisses and five hugs from all of us.'

'Why five hugs?' said Little Wool. 'There aren't five of them, are there?'

So they all counted up to see how many there were, and they found there were only four. Mary thought hard for a minute and then she said,

'One hug from each of them, and I expect the other is for me to give myself because of the party.'

'Of course,' said the twins.

Chapter Eight

Mary's party

The next day went very quickly on the whole. In the evening up went the doors, and Job called Mary to see how he had arranged the party. The twins longed to go too, but Mary said they must go into the corner and keep their backs turned till she came back or there wouldn't be a party at all.

On the table were piles of figs and cakes, and carrots, and in the centre the largest heap of all was made of cream buns. An empty bowl was by each place, and beside it Mary put a small paper parcel. Then she said that if Job wouldn't mind going away she would get ready herself.

Mary shut the door, and at the same moment a procession from Parlour Pit arrived.

First came Big Wool, holding Harrods' arm and walking carefully in step. Next came Bunch, but there wasn't much step about him, because he kept turning back longingly to look at his tree. Last of all came Friska. She had to be last because they thought Bunch might be troublesome. So Friska was prepared, and every time Bunch turned back she gave him a little shove with her head and said, 'Buns, Bunch,' and that sent him on again. Once in Nursery Pit, Friska locked the door and hid the key.

By this time the twins were so tired of the corner and keeping their backs turned that they were definitely peeping, and as soon as they saw the others arriving they backed out of their corner.

'Where's Mary?' asked Big Wool. 'Why is she not here to receive us? Or is it a mistake, and there isn't a party at all?'

'Oh, yes, it's a party,' said the twins, 'and Mary's gone in to get it ready, and she said we must stand with our backs turned to the door till she told us we needn't or there wouldn't be a party at all.'

All the bears hastily turned and faced the wall, and when Mary opened the door she saw six obedient backs.

'Good evening,' said Mary.

All the backs turned quickly into faces, and all the faces stared and stared at Mary. Because Mary was in full dress. She wore her swimming costume, and the sailor hat perched over one ear, and round her throat, being unable to tie a bow, she had wound the blue satin ribbon. But it was the swimming costume that held them spellbound. Friska, especially, thought she had never seen anyone look so smart before.

'First a red stripe, then a white,' she murmured to herself. Her eyes travelled upwards and fell on the ribbon.

'Oh, Mary,' she said, 'is your throat sore?'

'Not at all, thank you,' said Mary, 'I am only wearing my party bow.'

'I beg your pardon,' said Friska. Mary bowed.

'Will you come in?' she said. 'The party has begun.'

She went and climbed onto her stool. It was a tall stool and made her sit quite a lot higher than the others, which was very satisfactory. Big Wool sat on her right and Friska on her left. Bunch sat as near the cream buns as possible. Mary said, 'Will you pass your bowls for milk and sugar, please?' Big Wool's was the first to arrive.

'How many lumps?' said Mary.

'Three,' said Big Wool, with great restraint.

'Three for manners and four for a treat,' said Mary.

When Bunch's turn came he said, 'Three for manners and twenty for me,' but Mary took no notice and gave him the same as the others. Every time she put the sugar into one of their bowls, she popped a lump into her own mouth just to be sure it wasn't turning to salt.

Just at first no one spoke much, but when some of the piles had got lower Mary told them all about her svisit.

'I can speak English,' she said, and she told them about 'God save the Queen', and how they must always stand up and salute when it was said. After a few practices they all learnt to do it very well, and now and then, during tea, so as to be sure they wouldn't forget it, Mary said, 'God Save the Queen' and they all had to stand to attention.

'And did you always wear those beautiful clothes?' inquired Friska.

'No, only swimming and at parties.'

Friska looked horrified. 'Not swimming, Mary. You didn't get those stripes wet, did you?'

'Oh, yes,' said Mary, 'you see, it's a swimming costume. Everybody wears them.'

'But wasn't yours the smartest?' asked Friska.

'Much,' said Mary.

Now Mary had been so busy talking and pouring out that she had really eaten much less than the others, and she had not yet had one single cream bun. She had counted Bunch eating five, and now only one was left, and Bunch had his eye on it. Swallowing his last mouthful as fast as he could, he

put out his paw to take it.

'God Save the Queen,' said Mary quickly. Back Bunch's paw had to come, and up to his head it had to go.

It was the rule that no bear could lower his paw from the salute till Mary took her own down. All had their eyes fixed on Mary except Bunch, who had his fixed on the cream bun. Still with her hand at the salute Mary said,

'And please pass me that cream bun. I have not had one yet – "God save the Queen!"' she ended quickly, as she saw Bunch's paw begin to move. So Mary got her bun, and Bunch watched her eat it gloomily.

'None of you have opened your parcels yet!' said Mary.

They had been so busy eating that they hadn't even noticed that they had parcels, so now there was a great crackling of paper and exclamations of delight. Because they were very nice paper hats – just the right one for each bear.

Big Wool felt this was the time for a slight speech, so rapping on the table, she stood up.

'Bears and cubs,' she began, 'I think you would all like me to offer our thanks to Mary Plain for giving us such a – er – pleasanterable party. I have enjoyed it, I am sure we all have enjoyed it.'

'And Bunch has just enjoyed the last carrot,' wailed Little Wool.

Big Wool glared. 'Silence there,' she growled, and Little Wool made himself as small as possible.

'We are glad to welcome Mary back,' continued Big Wool, 'and at the same time, alas! we have to bid her farewell. For she is again to go out into the world. One never can tell – one never can tell. The outside world is very big, and Mary is very small, and she is going a long way off. I repeat, as I repeated before, "You never can tell."' A tear trickled down Friska's nose. 'But, though we cannot tell, we can always hope, and we do hope, and we must go on hoping that our hopes will come true.'

Here Big Wool sat down, leaving everyone a little uncertain as to what they had hoped for.

'And now shall I show you a magic trick?' said Mary.

'Please, please,' cried all the bears.

Mary took from a small box by her side two tin watches. First she walked to where Little Wool sat and, removing his bonnet, hid the watch in it, and replaced the hat on his head.

'Ow!' said Little Wool, 'it's tickling my head.'

'Ssh!' said Mary sternly.

Then going back to her place she opened the box, put the second watch inside it, and closed down the lid.

'Now,' she said, 'I shall say a magic word over this box, and then I shall ask one of you to tell me where the watch inside has disappeared to. Now, ready!'

All the bears held their breath.

'Cabra!' said Mary, who could only remember part of the word.

A complete silence reigned, broken only by Bunch, who, at the point of suffocation, was forced to take a deep breath.

'Cabra!' said Mary again, and dropped behind the table with the box. A moment later she reappeared, still with the box.

'Now,' she said, 'I will show you this box is empty – completely empty.'

She opened it and held it up. The bears gasped; the watch had gone, completely. It just wasn't there.

'Marvellous!' said Friska, in a throaty whisper. 'Marvellous!'

Mary bowed. All the bears bowed back.

'Now,' said Mary, 'not one of you can guess where I shall find that watch, can you?'

Dead silence.

'Very well,' said Mary grandly, 'I will show you.' She marched down the table, removed Little Wool's bonnet, took out the watch and held it up.

'There!' she said triumphantly. 'There is the watch!'

Lots of 'clever Marys' were shouted, and Mary bowed.

'The party is now over,' she said, 'so goodbye.'

The bears at once began to leave.

Big Wool asked if she might have a word in private with Mary, so together they went into a corner. Big Wool cleared her throat and said, 'I only want to say, Mary, that I trust you would not consider appearing in the Pit during the daytime in those clothes. I should not at all like you to draw attention.'

'What is a tension?' asked Mary.

'Well, it means making people notice you,' explained Big Wool.

'Oh, but I like people to notice me,' said Mary.

'Yes, yes,' said Big Wool, 'I have no objection to their noticing you, but I would not care for them to notice the costume – at least, not on you.'

'But the Fancy-Coat-Lady said it was a perfect fit,' said Mary.

'That may be. But it is not fitting to wear even a perfect pit in a fit,' said Big Wool, getting a little muddled.

Mary was getting a little muddled too, so it was a good thing that Job came along just then and said it was bedtime, and would they please hurry to their dens.

'Did you like my party?' said Mary, as she and the twins snuggled up together in the straw.

'Yes,' said Little Wool, 'wasn't it exciting when you found the watch you had hidden in my bonnet? Is it very grown-up to give a party, Mary Plain?'

'Yes,' said Mary, 'especially in a swimming costume.'

Chapter Nine

About the barber and the journey

Punctually at eleven o'clock the next morning the Owl Man came to take Mary to the barber's. She was feeling a bit nervous inside, but she tried not to show it.

It was not far to the barber's, and the tram stopped just opposite the door. There was some writing on the glass of the door, and the Owl Man said it was 'English spoken', which meant the barber could talk English. Mary said it to herself all the way upstairs.

'I know English already,' she announced.

'Do you?' said the Owl Man. 'How much?'

'English spoken,' said Mary.

'Good! What else?'

'God save the Queen,' said Mary, at the salute.

'Splendid, splendid!' said the Owl Man. 'You'll get on like a house on fire, I can see.'

As Mary got near the top of the stairs, the idea of being trimmed upset her more and more. 'Will it hurt much?' she whispered, tugging at the Owl Man's arm as he opened the door of the barber's room.

'Hurt? What could hurt?'

'The scissors,' said Mary, 'being trimmed with scissors. Will they stick them into me all over?'

'Good gracious me!' said the Owl Man, 'it's not that sort of trimming. The kind of trimming they do in barbers' shops is cutting.'

Mary thought to herself that sounded even worse, and she wore a very anxious expression as she was lifted onto a revolving stool and a large white cape was tied round her.

The barber picked up the scissors and said, 'I will now proceed. I think we had better have a bit off the ears to begin with, and then pass on to the body.'

Mary clapped her paws over her ears. 'No, no, not my ears!' she cried, struggling to get off the stool and

getting more and more entangled in the cape. 'Don't let him cut my ears, please, Owl Man!'

'Steady, Mary, steady!' said the Owl Man. 'It's only the long hair on your ears he wants to cut off, so it will be nice and smooth and smart. You don't want to go to England and have people say how untidy Swiss bears are, do you?' And he went on talking like this till Mary quieted down, and then the barber very kindly clipped a bit at the back of her head, just to get her used to it, and Mary found she didn't mind a bit.

She really looked very sleek when he had finished. She gazed at herself admiringly in the mirror.

'Couldn't I have a little white path down my head like yours?' she asked the Owl Man, but he assured her that the best bears didn't wear paths.

'It wasn't so bad after all, was it?' said the Owl Man when they were on their way home.

'No,' said Mary; 'shall we go again this afternoon?'

'I think once is enough for one day,' said the Owl Man.

The twins rushed up when Mary got back to the Pit. 'I've been barbered,' she said, 'aren't I smooth?'

'Your coat's all flat like the floor,' said Little Wool.

But it didn't stay flat for long, because Mary started a race round the pit, which is very unsmoothing to fur – especially when you get two cousins on top of you.

It seemed like a dream to think of going away that very night, and Mary wondered if it could really be true, because she went to bed with the others exactly the same as usual. The only difference was that she solemnly shook hands all round, and Big Wool told her to be good and mind her manners, and Friska begged her to keep up her counting and not forget all her Swiss, and Bunch said he'd be obliged if she'd bring him back some English cream buns – largest size.

Mary was tight asleep when she felt a shake and heard Job say, 'Come along, Mary, time to go – wake up!' She had been tucked in warmly between the cubs, and it felt very chilly to be taken out.

'Wake up, Mary,' he said again as he slipped her collar on; 'if you don't look sharp the Owl Man will be off without you.'

The Owl Man was waiting in a taxi, Mary was lifted in, and almost before she could wave to Job she was off.

Mary had never been in a station before, and she thought it a very big and quite frightening place. When they stood on the platform and a huge black train came thundering in, she got really upset and, bracing all four legs firmly, she refused to budge. In vain the Owl Man pulled and argued. Mary just said, 'I would rather stay in Berne, thank you.' Finally, he was so afraid the train would start without them that he picked Mary up, and tucking her, kicking, under his arm, he put her in the corridor – just as the train started. Mary promptly fell flat on her back, as she was not expecting it. 'What a rude train!' she said, as she picked herself up.

The Owl Man was quite hot and bothered by the scene on the platform, and he hurried Mary along to their compartment, which was the last in the carriage. But Mary took one look and refused to go in. 'I will not, I will not go in that box!' she screamed. It was the first time she had ever been really naughty, and he knew it was partly fright, but he felt the quickest way to bring her to her senses was to leave her alone, so he went into the compartment and said, 'Very well – you can stay

outside, all alone, till you can behave yourself,' and he shut the door.

Then he sat on the edge of his bunk and mopped his forehead and wished Mary were safely back in her pit.

The growls stopped directly he shut the door – only a succession of bumps went on outside, which was Mary falling down because she had not got her train legs yet. Presently even the bumps stopped, and at first the Owl Man was glad, and then he began to feel a little uneasy. You never could tell what Mary would think of doing next, and he wondered what she was up to.

He did not wonder long! A piercing shriek sent him flying to the door, and as he opened it he heard something like this: 'Fire! Wild animals – (shriek) – in my compartment – (shriek). Zoo! (shriek) Fire! (shriek),' and down the corridor came an old lady. Her grey hair streamed behind her, and she held her skirt high above her thin knees. With her mouth wide open she advanced on the Owl Man, 'Zoo! Fire! Help!' she screamed, as she flung herself into his arms. 'Save me, oh, save me! Zoo!' The Owl Man held her up and patted her soothingly. 'There, there,' he said, 'there, there, I beg that you will not distress yourself, Madam. I can assure you that the small bear is perfectly harmless. Mary, Mary,' he called.

Mary emerged from a door at the other end of the corridor, and directly the old lady saw her she started screaming again, and hid behind the Owl Man.

Another door opened and a man's head popped out. 'What is all this dreadful noise?' he asked.

'Save me! Wild animal! Help!' shouted the old lady from behind the Owl Man. Turning his head, the man saw Mary approaching, and he banged the door shut.

The others had now reached the farther end of the corridor, for as soon as Mary appeared the old lady had begun pulling the Owl Man backwards, and though she was not young, there was nothing old about her pull.

'Will you kindly let go of my coat?' said the Owl Man, who was getting quite annoyed. 'It's ridiculous to make so much fuss over a small harmless bear – a perfectly friendly bear.'

'I don't wish it to be friendly with me,' panted the old lady.

By this time Mary was level with their compartment door. The Owl Man pointed at it and said, in a voice of thunder, 'In you get, Mary, in double quick time, or you'll be sorry!' and Mary, with one look at his face, obeyed like a lamb.

The Owl Man closed the door, with the old lady still fastened on behind him like a tail. Then he shook himself free, and tried to be polite, because after all, Mary was his bear.

'Now, Madam, if you will permit me, I will accompany you back to your own compartment. I am more than sorry this should have happened.'

Then he returned to his own compartment, and found Mary sitting on the edge of the bunk looking quite sheepish.

'Well, Mary Plain,' he said, 'I hope you are proud of yourself.'

'Whatever was the matter with that old lady?' asked Mary. 'I only thought it was your door, and when it wasn't, I said I was tired of being in the corridor, so could I sleep in her bed with her?'

The Owl Man, tired as he was, had to smile, but he quickly put on a stern face again and said, 'Now, see here, Mary Plain, you have given me a whole lot of trouble –'

'Was it a trouble when the old lady hugged you?' asked Mary in an interested voice. 'I thought it was kind to hug.'

'Don't interrupt me, please, Mary. As I was saying, you have given me a lot of trouble, and if this happens again, back you go to Berne by the next train – understand me?'

'I do,' said Mary.

'Either you behave from now on, or home you go – *at once*!'

Mary stared at him.

'Are you cross?' she inquired. 'Your face is all red.'

'I should think it would be, and yes, I am cross – and it all depends on you how soon I stop being cross – see?'

Mary saw. Sometimes she could see quite well, and when she was told to get up into the top berth and go to sleep, she went without a word.

In the middle of the night the Owl Man was disturbed. He heard a movement and switched on the light, and there, in the air, were a pair of furry legs – kicking wildly. Mary was suspended from the strap of the upper berth.

'What in the world are you doing, Mary?' he asked.

'I want to get down because I'm thirsty,' said Mary, 'but I've lost my way. Where has the staircase gone?'

The Owl Man helped her down and gave her a drink, and very soon all was quiet again.

Morning came, and together they had breakfast, and Mary had a whole thermos of milk to herself.

'Will that be the only night in the train?' she enquired, as they spun across Paris in a taxi.

'Yes, thank goodness!' said the Owl Man, and Mary could see from his face that he was glad.

Chapter Ten

Which is still about the journey

The Owl Man had taken seats in the 'Golden Arrow' because fewer people travel by that train and he thought it would be less crowded.

The attendant showed them to two corner seats, and they were really quite private. Mary was very impressed by the chairs, and stroked them admiringly. The Owl Man explained about its being velvet, as he lifted her onto hers.

Mary felt very grand.

'Am I a hostess, then?' she asked.

The Owl Man smiled and said, 'That's right, and

I am the party.'

'Are you all the party I've got?' said Mary, looking quite disappointed.

'I'm afraid so, you'll just have to make the best of me,' said the Owl Man. 'Now, look here, I'm just going to get a paper, so sit still till I come back, there's a good cub.'

From her seat Mary could see all the way down the carriage, and just as the Owl Man disappeared, a lady came through the door at the farther end of the carriage. So there was some more party after all.

Mary slipped off her chair and went forward with paw outstretched.

'I'm so glad you've come,' she said, 'because the Owl Man doesn't make a very big party all by himself.'

The lady was so surprised that she dropped one of the wraps she was carrying, and by the time she and Mary had both tried to pick it up, and had bumped their heads together and then said, 'I beg your pardon,' several other people had arrived. Mary was busily greeting them when the Owl Man came back. He saw Mary's chair was empty and his heart sank, and then he saw a little crowd at the other end of the saloon, and felt sure it was because of Mary.

He was quite right.

'And I made a pome and I have a swimming costume,' she was saying, 'and do sit down. There's lots of chairs and they're all blue velvet, and blue is my best colour, and then red and then yellow.'

The Owl Man hurried up.

'I'm so sorry,' he said apologetically, 'I do hope she hasn't been a nuisance, but I just ran out to get a paper.'

'Not at all,' said a charming young lady in a very blue hat, 'she's been most entertaining. It isn't often one has the chance to travel with a bear, you see.'

'Thank heaven!' said the Owl Man fervently.

'Is it tiring?' asked the young lady aside.

The Owl Man didn't answer, but he just rolled his eyes up and the young lady seemed to understand at once what he meant.

'Now, come along, Mary Plain,' he said, 'you must come back to your corner, and sit still. You know you aren't supposed to run about all over the carriage like this. I've only paid for those two chairs in the corner and that's all that belongs to us.'

'But didn't you pay for this lady's seat?' enquired Mary.

The Owl Man looked a little embarrassed and shook his head.

'Oh,' said Mary, 'and she's my party!'

At this both the Owl Man and the young lady burst out laughing. Then the Owl Man took Mary firmly by the paw and led her back to their seats, and luckily lunch was brought in just then, so Mary was kept busy for some time because she said 'Yes, please' to everything all the way through.

After the pudding, the Owl Man went into the passage to find a book he wanted which was in his suitcase, and when he came back he could hardly see Mary, because she was hidden behind a pile of things she'd said 'Yes please' to. There was a basket of fruit, cheese, biscuits, butter and a plate piled high with chocolates.

'Great heavens! Mary Plain,' exclaimed the Owl Man, 'what in the world have you been doing?'

'Just saying "Yes, please",' said Mary.

The Owl Man had to collect the attendant and explain how difficult it was for Mary ever to say 'No, thank you!' and the man was a kind man and understood about bears, and said he would take all the things away again, which he did.

And then Mary had a sleep. When she woke up she found the lady in the blue hat had moved to a chair near the Owl Man's and was talking to him in a low voice.

'And then I looked over the edge of the pit,' she was saying, 'and there was a large bear lying on its back, holding its toes and hanging its tongue out.'

'Big Wool resting,' said Mary, sitting up.

'Hello, awake again?' said the lady. 'Big Wool is a splendid name for a bear, I think: and then there was a black one in a corner asleep, and a brown one wandering about looking quite dull.'

'Harrods was the asleep one,' explained Mary, 'and Friska only looks happy when it's lesson time.'

'Really! She must be very clever.'

'Yes,' said Mary, 'she teaches me. I can count up to five,' she added modestly.

The young lady opened her eyes wide. 'Well, isn't that marvellous?' she said. 'Now, I wonder if you can tell me the name of the last bear in that pit. He has a big ruff of fur round his neck, and he sits on a branch of the tree and claps his paws.'

'Bunch,' said Mary, 'waiting for carrots.'

'Or sugar,' said the Owl Man. Mary looked at him.

'You always keep some special Bunch sugar in your pocket, don't you?' she said wistfully.

And then a lovely thing happened, for the Owl Man said, 'Open your mouth and shut your eyes and you shall have a nice surprise,' and when Mary had done both these things there were two lumps of sugar in her mouth. They all laughed, and then the lady continued.

'Afterwards I went to another pit, and there were two very, very old bears with not many teeth.'

'Lady Grizzle and Alpha,' said Mary respectfully; 'they are very old and clever and we only see them on St Bruin's Day, so I don't know them well.'

'That's interesting,' said the lady, and hoped Mary would tell her about St Bruin's Day, but instead she said eagerly,

'And where did you go after?'

'Well,' said the lady slowly, 'I went on a bit and then I came to another pit.'

'Yes, yes,' said Mary, beginning to wriggle in her chair. 'Go on, go on!'

'And in that pit there was one small bear having a bath, with a black coat.'

'Little Wool,' said Mary. 'Go on, go on!'

'And another brown one climbing the tree.'

'Yes, yes,' said Mary in an agony of expectation, 'and go on!'

'Let me see, *was* there another?' said the lady who was quite a tease.

Mary's face fell, and she sat quite still.

'Oh, of course,' said the lady, 'now I remember, there was a browny-grey bear with pointed ears, a little smaller than the others, who did the most beautiful jumps.'

'Me, me,' bounced Mary, 'that was me!'

The young lady fell back in her chair. 'You? You? But I don't believe you can jump!'

So then Mary had to get down off her chair to show her that she could, but unfortunately she had forgotten about the train, so she landed quite flat on her face. The Owl Man picked her up and gave her a rub, and the lady said she did hope it hadn't hurt much.

'Just my dinner place, a little,' said Mary, stroking it.

'Do you think it's going to be rough?' the lady asked the Owl Man as she got up to go back to her own seat.

'Well, it's not very hopeful. The papers say "sea rough to very rough".'

'Isn't she a good sailor?'

'I hope so, but she's never crossed before. We must hope for the best!' He smiled and bowed as the young lady went off. Calais was very exciting. They walked up a steep plank onto the boat and Mary could see all the water underneath.

'Is that the C?' she asked.

'That's right,' said the Owl Man, holding her paw tightly.

When he got on board the first thing he did was to say, 'Is Steward Saunders here?' Saunders was a great friend of his, whom he had known in the war, and he always looked after him very well. He found the Owl Man two chairs in a good position on the upper deck and got them settled.

At first Mary walked about a bit. She peeped round the corner and then came back and said, 'There's a very untidy gentleman round the corner.'

It was a rough day, so the Owl Man knew at once what she meant, and said, 'Yes, and it's very, very wrong to be untidy on the deck; you must always go to the side of the ship.'

Mary listened gravely. She played about for a few minutes and then she came running back to the Owl Man.

'I feel –' she began.

The Owl Man hurried her to the side of the boat.

'Am I going to be untidy?' inquired Mary, much interested.

'That's a question you alone can answer,' said the Owl Man, 'but I hope not.' They went on leaning over for a bit and nothing happened, so they went back to their seats.

Mary hummed a little song and then said, 'I feel –' In a twinkling the Owl Man was back at the side of the boat with a sympathetic hand on her forehead.

'Why do you hold my head?' asked Mary.

'Don't you like it?' said the Owl Man.

'No,' said Mary.

The Owl Man took his hand away. Mary gazed downwards.

'Does any one live in the C?' she asked.

'Only fishes,' said the Owl Man.

'And what are their names?' asked Mary next.

'There are so many different kinds,' said the Owl Man. 'There is sole, and trout, and hake, and salmon, and halibut, and cod, and –'

'Do cods wear swimming costumes?' interrupted Mary.

The Owl Man chuckled. 'No, you see all fish wear slippery skins especially made for the water.'

'Cods, too?'

'Yes, all the same.'

'I should like to meet a cod,' said Mary.

Just then Saunders came up. 'Getting on all right?' he asked.

'Yes,' said the Owl Man. 'Had one or two frights, but nothing came of them. I think the thing is to keep them interested talking and give them no time to think.'

'That's right,' said Saunders. 'I've just got to run down and see about some luggage in the hold. Shall I take her along and relieve you a bit?'

'Thanks,' said the Owl Man. 'You'd like that, wouldn't you, Mary?'

'Yes, please,' said Mary.

But before they went down Saunders had to take a message, so Mary went with him and visited the Captain in his little glass box with his enormous wheel. He had a kind face, and when Mary told him she was used to driving the Owl Man's car, he let her drive the boat for just five seconds, and that is probably the first

and the last time that the *Canterbury* has ever been steered by a bear.

Then they went down a lot of stairs, and at last they got to a square place piled full of luggage. Nearby was a huge heap of bags, and Saunders told Mary that every bag was full of letters going to England, and then he was called away and Mary was left alone.

She waited for a bit and then began climbing about the pile of bags, and then she got tired of waiting, so she curled up between the top bags and fell asleep.

And she didn't wake till she felt herself suddenly being shaken about. For a moment she was upside down, and then a bag slipped and she was right side up again – wedged between two bags of letters which were hugging her very tightly.

All around her and the bags was a huge net, and inside her was a strange rocking feeling.

At first she wondered if she was in a dream, and then she thought she must be flying, and when she looked over the edge her heart stood quite still, because it was true. She was flying – high,

high up in the air, and far down below she could see the boat with little people moving about on it. Above her head was a huge iron kind of bird which held the net in its claws. In fact, Mary couldn't look up or down without hating it, so she closed her eyes very tightly instead and was glad of the affectionate bags.

Though it seemed simply ages to Mary, it was only a few seconds that they were up in the air, and then they began to drop, down, down, swinging backwards and forwards, as they went, a really horrid feeling. And the end was the most alarming of all, for the net just opened itself, and out fell all the bags – and Mary.

Luckily she had been at the top, so lots of bags fell first and made a sort of mattress for her to fall on when her turn came.

As she picked herself up and stood up in the middle of the bags, several men who were standing round began rubbing their eyes. Could they be mad, or was that really a live bear standing there?

Mary stared back and realized this must be England. One man with gold buttons down his jacket ran off and brought some more, and presently there were twelve gold-buttoned men all standing in a row and staring at Mary.

'God save the Queen!' said Mary, saluting smartly.

All the men stood with their arms very stiff down at their sides and nobody spoke. There was a pause.

'English spoken,' said Mary pleasantly.

The fattest man stepped forward at once and said,

'That's a good thing, for now perhaps you'll be able to answer a few questions.'

But to Mary it sounded like, 'Thisaguthinfonoprapsyulbeabtoanserafuquesuns,' because she could only understand Swiss.

She shook her head and said, 'I am afraid I don't know those kind of words, but will you please find the Owl Man for me, because I want him.'

And then it was the men's turn to shake their heads. And just when they were all trying to decide what to do, the Owl Man hurried up with Saunders after him. He looked quite white.

'Mary Plain!' he exclaimed, 'where in the name of thunder have you been?'

'I haven't been in any name,' said Mary, 'I've been in with those bags, and not on purpose, neither.'

'She must have gone to sleep among the mail,' said Saunders. 'Then, of course, she got swung over in the net along with the bags.'

'I did,' said Mary, 'but I don't want to do it again, please.'

'I bet you don't,' said the Owl Man, who had gone pink again with relief at finding Mary. 'Well, all's well that ends well. Come on, Mary, hang on to me and don't let go for one single second.'

The twelve buttoned men were still standing in a row staring, and still wondering if it were all a dream.

The Owl Man and Mary went into a long place with benches and more men with gold buttons standing behind them. One of them asked the Owl Man if he had anything to declare.

'Only this bear,' he said, pointing at Mary.

The man looked quite agitated, and had to go and talk to several other officers, and then he came back, had another stare at Mary, and said,

'That will be sevenpence halfpenny, please, sir.'

'God save the Queen!' said Mary.

This time they got into another train, and this time there were red velvet seats, and there was hot buttered toast to eat. The toast was extra buttery, and so was Mary when she had finished, because her chest stuck out a good deal and was very inviting to butter. The Owl Man had to use a whole handkerchief getting her clean.

'Will it be long now?' she asked him.

'Long before we arrive, do you mean?'

Mary nodded.

'No, only another hour,' said the Owl Man. Mary sighed happily.

'I feel –' she began.

'No you don't – nonsense, Mary!' interrupted the Owl Man quickly.

'But I *do* feel glad I've come,' said Mary, getting it out at last. The Owl Man groaned.

'Is that what you've been trying to say ever since we left Calais, Mary Plain?' he asked.

'Yes,' said Mary, 'but you never let me finish, did you?'

Chapter Eleven

Which a bus starts,
and the Queen ends

Mary had an excellent night. She slept in a tiny empty room opening out of the Owl Man's, in the small flat which was his home.

Next morning he said that he thought the first thing to do was for Mary to have a swim, as she was a bit grimy after the journey and she must be looking her very best for the show next day.

The Owl Man decided to go by bus, as his car had not yet arrived, so they went and stood at the corner of Baker Street for a No. 30 to come along.

When the bus drew up there was a slight difficulty about getting on, as the conductor said Mary didn't come under the heading of 'small dogs under proper control'. This was quite true, but Mary had her collar on, and, as the Owl Man pointed out, though she wasn't a dog she was certainly under proper control, and she was perfectly accustomed to travelling in trams and trains.

'But not in a bus,' said Mary excitedly. But the Owl Man coughed very loudly, so luckily no one heard her.

'Orl right,' said the conductor at last, 'take 'er up aloft, but if there's any complaints, mind, off you gets.'

So the Owl Man pushed Mary in front of him up the stairs. Upstairs Mary and the Owl Man were in the front seat, and Mary was enjoying it very much.

'Aren't I tall?' she said, looking over the side. 'Why, look at all those hats walking about!' The Owl Man explained that it was because she was so high up, and that underneath the hats were the people that wore them.

No one seemed to object to Mary except one elderly gentleman who made a clicking noise with his teeth and murmured, 'The Zoo is the Zoo – but bears on buses! (Click, click.)'

The Owl Man and Mary changed buses at Hyde Park Corner, and a No. 9 took them to Prince's Gate, and from there they walked across the park to the swimming place.

Here a new difficulty arose. Mixed swimming was allowed at certain hours, but just now it was divided up into 'Ladies' and 'Gentlemen', and the man in charge was not sure which heading bears would come under. He decided to take no risks, and he went indoors and fetched a small board and on it he wrote, 'Bears only', and stuck it in the water a little beyond the ladies' part.

There was quite a fuss when Mary realized she had forgotten her swimming costume, but the Owl Man told her bears were not allowed to wear them in England *ever*, so Mary was pacified.

All the ladies were very excited about seeing a bear bathe, but they were also glad there was a rope dividing Mary's section from theirs, and they stayed well on their own side of it and watched.

Now, being watched always went to Mary's head, and, finding a kind of bar between two poles close to the rope, she climbed up on it and did some excellent dives. The ladies clapped and shouted and Mary felt no end of a success, and did more dives. Finally she

got so excited that she forgot to remember which direction to swim in under the water, and she came up right in the middle of a bunch of ladies, giving one of them a severe shove with her head.

'Ladies only!' shrieked the outraged female, and all the others started screaming and shouting too. One of them sank with fright and had to be rescued by the attendant, and the Owl Man said Mary must stop swimming and come out at once.

So Mary plunged out, and she and the Owl Man walked home across the park, and Mary shook herself and rolled on the grass to get dry and ran races with herself and always won.

Mary ran loose in the park, but as soon as they got to the gates the Owl Man put her lead on again, as he did not want to risk mislaying her. The traffic was very bad at Marble Arch; Mary did not at all like crossing the street, and several times the Owl Man had almost to drag her across. He was quite breathless when they got to the other side.

'You mustn't pull like that, Mary Plain,' he said, 'you'll have us under one of those buses if you're not careful.'

'I don't like it,' said Mary. 'All the cars and buses are running after me and trying to catch me, and

I don't like it.'

'Well, this afternoon we'll go and collect my car, and then, thank goodness, there will be no need to go out in anything else,' said the Owl Man.

After lunch and a rest, they set out again, this time by tube. Tubes are very hot places, and the Owl Man noticed that Mary got quieter and quieter, so when she said, 'Do you think the twins are happy without me?' he got out at the next station, which was Oxford Circus.

Once out of the tube, Mary forgot all about the twins. They walked down Regent Street towards Charing Cross, and Mary stopped to look in nearly all the shop windows. One shop had a stuffed bear in it, and Mary tried to talk to it, but she didn't know about windows so she walked straight up against the glass and got a bad bump. The Owl Man explained that though you could see through glass you couldn't walk through, and also that the little brown bear couldn't talk because he was a toy bear.

'But he looked at me, and I *think* he winked,' said Mary.

The Owl Man said, 'Come on now, Mary,' and pulled, but Mary stood with all four legs braced and refused to budge.

The Owl Man knew the only thing to do was to draw her attention away, so he said in an excited voice, 'That's the Fancy-Coat-Lady,' and, though he knew quite well she was in Switzerland, he dashed down the street dragging Mary with him.

And Mary was so delighted at the thought of seeing her dear Fancy-Coat-Lady that she ran too. Safely out of the sight of the toy bear the Owl Man stopped running, and said he was afraid he had made a mistake, and it wasn't her after all.

'Then can I go back and see the little bear again?' said Mary, beginning to stiffen her legs again, but the Owl Man said, 'No, we'll go in here and get some tea. Wouldn't you like a cream bun?' And Mary unbraced at once and followed him in obediently.

In this shop she saw éclairs for the first time. She couldn't quite decide whether she liked éclairs or meringues best, so she had to have first one and then the other to make sure, and by the time she finally decided on meringues she had eaten twelve éclairs and thirteen meringues.

They then continued their walk, and when they got to Trafalgar Square Mary was very interested in the lions when they passed them.

'They are put there to guard Lord Nelson – that man who is standing on the top of the pole,' explained the Owl Man.

'Is he pretending to be a bird?' asked Mary. 'And isn't he very lonely all alone up there?'

'I never thought about it,' said the Owl Man.

'I'll just run up and ask him, shall I?' said Mary, making for the column, but luckily her lead was on, so the Owl Man pulled her back and said she would be arrested if she started climbing public monuments in London.

'What does "arrested" mean?' said Mary.

'It means that gentleman with the helmet would come along and take you off with him.'

Mary stared hard at the policeman standing close to the column.

'Isn't he kind then?' she asked.

'I'm sure he'd be kind – policemen always are,' said the Owl Man, 'but when you break the law –'

'But I shouldn't break it, climbing it,' interrupted Mary, 'it's made of stone.'

'Breaking the law means doing things you are forbidden to,' explained the Owl Man. 'And when you do that you get popped into prison.'

'Isn't it a nice place?'

'Well, I don't fancy you'd enjoy it much.'

'Wouldn't there be no figs, or cream buns, or milk, or meringues?'

'None, only bread and water,' said the Owl Man.

'Then I shan't go,' decided Mary, and gave up all idea of swarming up the Nelson column.

It took some time to collect the car at the station, and when at last they got away they were held up by a traffic jam just outside. The Owl Man stood up because he heard some shouting, and then he saw that at the corner of the street a crowd of people were cheering and waving.

'It's the Queen!' he said. 'Up you hop, Mary,' and he held her up on the side of the car, so she could see right over all the cars in front.

'God save the Queen!' shouted Mary, and just as she spoke, the Queen, who was waving to left and right, waved in Mary's direction.

'I called "God save the Queen" and she heard me,' she said happily.

'How do you know?' asked the Owl Man.

'Because she waved a "thank you" at me,' said Mary. So there was no doubt about it. She had.

Chapter Twelve

The show

As the show was to open at twelve and all competitors were requested to be at Earl's Court by eleven o'clock, the Owl Man and Mary set off in good time.

She was looking in excellent condition, with her coat thoroughly brushed. The Owl Man had given her a tin of biscuits to take, in case there was any difficulty about her dinner. The biscuits made a rattly noise when Mary shook the tin, and the rattle made her wonder what kind of biscuits they were.

As Mary had never been exhibited before, the Owl Man thought he had better explain about her being put in an enclosure.

'I would like to stay outside with you, thank you,' said Mary firmly.

'But you can't do that, Mary Plain,' said the Owl Man. 'You've come halfway across Europe for this show, and one of the rules is that all competitors have to be in an enclosure. Who knows? You might win a rosette!'

'What is that?' said Mary, who liked winning things.

'Well, some very important people go round and they have three little badges of coloured ribbons – white, green, and blue; and when they have decided which is the very best animal shown, they give it the white ribbon to wear; the next best gets the green, and the last best, the blue ribbon,' explained the Owl Man.

They arrived up at an entrance to Earl's Court labelled *Competitors Only*, and the Owl Man helped Mary out. They walked through a gate and down a passage, and then the Owl Man noticed that Mary had not got the biscuit tin.

'Mary,' he exclaimed, 'you've forgotten your biscuits!'

'Oh, no, I haven't,' said Mary.

'But where's the box?'

'I didn't like the rattle the biscuits made,' said Mary.

'How absurd!'

'So I stopped it,' said Mary.

'Well, you'll be sorry not to have them when lunchtime comes.'

'But I couldn't eat them twice, could I?' said Mary.

'Oh, Mary, Mary!' said the Owl Man.

Then they were stopped by a man who sat behind a table and worked a turnstile.

'Is this a competitor?' he asked.

'Yes,' said the Owl Man. So he handed them a beautiful pink ticket and they went clicking through the gate.

A tall thin man was telling the different people where to go, but it was quite a muddle, because so many would ask him all at once.

A lady with a large flop-eared rabbit tucked under each arm was asking where she could put them down quickly, because they were so heavy; while another very old lady, holding a birdcage with a parrot in it, clung to his arm.

'Would you be so very kind as to tell me where place Twenty-Seven is, please?'

'Please a poll – please a poll,' said the parrot.

And before the thin man could answer up came someone else leading a young seal who didn't care about shows and was saying so in a very loud voice.

Mary drew close to the Owl Man. 'Why does it make that rude noise?' she asked, and the Owl Man, shouting very loudly so as to be heard above the parrot and the seal, said, 'I can't think, Mary, but I wish he wouldn't.'

'My poor Philip, so tired!' said the owner of the parrot, 'and I should like the poor dear to have a quiet sleep before the judge comes round.'

'Good morning, all!' said Philip brightly.

'Honk,' roared the seal, who was called Bertha.

'Shut up, Bertha!' said its owner.

At last they all got sent off in the right directions, and then the Owl Man got a chance to ask where number Nineteen was.

'You come along with me,' said the tall thin man, 'I'll show you,' and he led them to a corner where two big enclosures stood.

On one side was a small enclosure and inside was a zebra. Mary was very interested about the stripes and wanted to know if they came off in the bath.

And on the other side was, funnily enough, another bear.

He belonged to a man who took him round to country shows, and he was getting old and a bit stiff in the joints. He reminded Mary a little bit of Harrods, only his eyes were not quite the same as hers.

'Good morning, bear,' said Mary conversationally. The old bear had a look at her and then sniffed and looked away again.

'I'm a bear too,' said Mary.

The old one sniffed again.

'A Swiss bear,' added Mary, and when she said that, the old fellow turned round and stared.

'My brother-in-law was Swiss,' he said; 'did you know him?'

'Was her name Harrods?' asked Mary, thinking of the likeness.

'My brother-in-law was not a she,' said the bear; '*he* was called Hoodwink.'

'No, I don't know him at all,' said Mary. 'Could he wink?'

The old bear turned an outraged back.

'Do you know what his name is?' Mary asked the Owl Man, and he told her it was Albert.

'How did you guess?' said Mary.

'Because he's got a notice fastened on to his enclosure which says, "Albert, Performing Bear; Owner, Alf Jones."'

'Have I got a notice too?' said Mary.

'Yes; yours says, "Mary Plain, from the famous bear pits at Berne, shown by Mr Owl Man."' Mary felt very proud about having a printed notice about herself, and asked if she could take it home with her after the show.

'Bunch hasn't got a notice about him, has he?' she said.

'No, he hasn't.'

'And he hasn't been to a show, has he?'

'No, he hasn't.'

'And he hasn't won a blue prize, has he?'

'No, he hasn't – and nor have you, Mary Plain,' said the Owl Man, who thought Mary was getting a little big-headed.

People were beginning to come round, looking at all the animals. When they saw, 'Albert, Performing Bear,' written up they all stood there to watch him perform.

And whatever Albert did Mary did a little better next door.

Presently, all the people that had been looking at Albert were standing outside Mary's enclosure, and laughing at her, and Albert was left quite alone, except for Alf Jones, who leaned against the enclosure and looked very glum.

You could see the judges getting nearer and nearer, and the Owl Man wished they would hurry up and see Mary at her best.

Then a terrible thing happened.

ALBERT
performing bear
owner:
Alf Jones

MARY PLAIN
from the famous
bear pits at Berne
shown by
Mr Owl Man

Mary got hiccups. She stood quite still. 'What is it?' she asked, and the Owl Man told her they were hiccups and she must hold her breath.

'I'll – *hic* – try,' said Mary, and she held it tight until her eyes began to bulge, and then she was sure it was cured, and she took a long breath to stop herself from bursting.

'They've gone!' she said.

'Hurrah!' said the Owl Man, much relieved.

'Yes, hur-*hic*,' said Mary.

'Dear, oh dear!' said the harassed Owl Man, 'what bad luck! Can't you think of anything that would stop them, Mary?'

'Shall I try a caramel – *hic*?' suggested Mary.

But that was no good; she nearly choked. The Owl Man looked at the judges; they only had to look at some guinea pigs and Albert before they arrived at Mary. He ground his teeth. It would be too much to bear if Mary said 'God save the *Hic*' to the judge.

'Try making her jump,' suggested an onlooker; 'give her a fright.' So the Owl Man got down on his hands and knees, and then bounced up suddenly and said, 'BOO!' But Mary only said, 'Aren't you feeling very well, Owl Man?'

Then the Owl Man remembered about water being a good thing, and several people ran to get a glass of water, and all of them told Mary which was the best way to swallow it. And when she had tried all the ways she put the glass down and stood very still in the middle of the enclosure, wearing that questioning look that means, 'Have they gone?'

All the people stood as still as still – you could have heard a pin drop.

At last the Owl Man said, 'Gone?' and his voice was full of hope.

'*Hic!*' answered Mary. Everyone groaned.

The judge was now on his way to Albert, and it seemed certain that Mary's chances were finished, when, after all, she got cured by a fright.

Bertha had wandered along till she was just opposite Mary's enclosure, and suddenly she found she could not see her owner anywhere and made the noise that seals only make when they are lost. Mary nearly jumped out of her skin, and did jump right out of her hiccups.

Then the judges came, and Mary showed off beautifully, jumping, marching, dancing, and winking with the greatest skill, and the judges were delighted with her.

They asked lots of questions, and the Owl Man said a lot of kind things about her, and Mary pretended not to hear.

Then the head one said, 'We have unanimously agreed that this young bear shall be awarded first prize.'

And all the crowd cheered and clapped, and the Owl Man said, 'Well done, Mary Plain!' and Mary got over-excited and said, 'Well done me!'

Then the judge said, 'I should like to pin the rosette on myself,' and the Owl Man said, 'Certainly, sir,' and unfastened the gate.

Mary got out and came up to the judge, and he said, 'Mary Plain, it gives me much pleasure to award you the first prize,' and Mary saluted and said, 'God save the Queen', which delighted the judge. He shook her warmly by the paw, and the crowd sang, 'For she's a jolly good fellow'.

Of course the prize couldn't be pinned on to Mary, because there was nothing but Mary herself to pin it to, so they tied it

round her neck on a piece of string, and Mary was very proud and pleased.

Now, it is very nice for the person who wins a prize, but it is never as much fun for the ones who don't.

Bertha said, 'Honk, honk, honk-honk-honk,' which meant she had already said that she didn't like shows; she had turned herself inside out and upside down doing tricks for the benefit of the judges, and she had not even won a blue ribbon. So this settled it – no more shows for her.

'Have you been to many?' said Mary.

'Seven,' said Bertha.

'But why aren't you wearing the rosettes you won?' asked Mary.

'I – er – I – er – haven't got them with me,' said Bertha hurriedly.

Meanwhile the parrot's birdcage had been covered with a green baize cloth. Philip had not even won the second prize, though, of course, he undoubtedly deserved the first. 'Judging is not what it used to be,' said the owner as she bent over the enclosure.

'Happy Poll, happy Poll,' said Philip from under the baize, so his mother thought it was time to go home.

Then the Owl Man led Mary off to find the car.

Halfway home Mary said, 'Bunch didn't have a notice about him, did he?'

'No, he didn't,' said the Owl Man.

'But I did, didn't I?'

'You did,' said the Owl Man.

'Bunch didn't win a white rosette, did he?'

'No, he didn't,' said the Owl Man.

'But I did, didn't I?'

'You did,' said the Owl Man humbly.

'So there!' said Mary Plain.

The Owl Man felt certain that he ought to stop Mary from becoming too big-headed, but when he turned to do it and saw her sitting beside him, with the rosette sitting on the very stuck-outest part of her chest, he just couldn't.

Chapter Thirteen

Mary svisits the Zoo

'I think we'll go to the Zoo today,' said the Owl Man next morning; 'it will be our only chance, because we start back tomorrow.'

'And what kind of a place is that?' asked Mary.

'Well, lots and lots of different kinds of animals live there, collected from all over the world.'

'Any Swiss bears?' asked Mary.

'I don't know about Swiss ones, but there are bears there all right,' said the Owl Man. 'Now, I'll go and ring up the garage and tell them to send the car round.'

When the Owl Man came back from the telephone Mary was standing in the hall.

'I'm ready,' she announced.

'I should think you are,' said the Owl Man. Because Mary wore her white rosette perched on top of her head with the string knotted under her chin, and the placard with her name on it was round her neck. The string of this was quite short, and the cardboard stuck out like a little shelf over her chest.

The Owl Man rubbed his chin. 'Why have you got those – er – decorations on, Mary?'

'Because if I don't wear them no one will know that I'm a first prize bear,' said Mary.

This was perfectly right. 'That's true,' said the Owl Man slowly, 'but all the same I think I should take them off if I were you, Mary Plain. You see, after all, most of the animals there haven't had a chance to go to a show and win a prize, and it might make them feel bad to see you wearing a rosette.'

Mary sighed, and took it off slowly. 'If only I had my swimming costume,' she said.

'Come on now,' said the Owl Man briskly. 'Once you get there you'll be so busy seeing and talking to all the different animals that you won't have time to miss your rosette or anything else,' and he bundled Mary into the car before she could think of something more to wear.

The Zoo was very exciting, and Mary's head whirled.

They went first to the monkey house, and Mary said she didn't like their old faces and the rude way they scratched themselves all the time.

Then they went on past the penguins, and Mary liked them a lot. They came hurrying towards them, holding up their black knickers as they always do.

One penguin, who wore a very smart tan and coloured scarf, was standing beside a very small black and white penguin, and he was stroking him over the head with his wings.

'Why do you do that?' asked Mary.

'Because he doesn't want to be adopted,' said the penguin, going on stroking.

'But must he be?' said Mary.

The penguin stopped and stared at Mary. 'But, of course,' he said. 'His mother and father are both dead, and therefore he must be adopted, and I am going on stroking him till he wants to be.'

Mary and the Owl Man moved on, Mary hoping very much that the small penguin would soon be willing.

They climbed a lot of steps, and there they were at the Mappin Terraces.

'You'll find some friends here, Mary,' said the Owl Man. 'This is where the bears live.'

Mary stared at the two bears who were lying on the edge of the big space which separated them from the railing.

'They're a long way off, aren't they?' she said. And she shouted, 'I've come a long way to see you, half in a train and half in a boat and half in a net.'

'You can't be three halves, Mary,' murmured the Owl Man.

'I *can* be,' said Mary, 'because I was.'

Then one of the bears yawned, and Mary, encouraged by this sign, shouted, 'What are your names?'

The yawny bear said, 'We are called Brownie and Doris.'

'I have got two names,' said Mary; 'would you like to guess what they are?'

'No,' said Brownie, 'but perhaps the twins next door might like to know them.'

'The twins?' shrieked Mary, rushing to the next division.

'But it isn't,' she said flatly, as she saw two large elderly bears lying asleep.

'You didn't think he meant Marionetta and Little Wool, did you, Mary?' said the Owl Man.

'But, of course!' said Mary; 'he said the twins.'

'But twins can happen more than once,' said the Owl Man.

'I wish they hadn't happened here,' said Mary, who was bitterly disappointed.

They moved on to the next lot. Of the three bears living here, the most interesting was 'Tarpot' Nellie, who was called this because she had fallen into a pot of tar when she was a baby.

'I should have chosen a pot of jam if it had been me,' said Mary as they went on to the polar bears.

'What smart white bears!' she exclaimed. 'Have they had so many baths that they've become white?'

The Owl Man laughed and said no, it was because they were a special sort of bear who lived in a country of ice and snow.

The keeper was standing near by, and he came up and told them about the polar bears. They were called Babs and Sam and Elisabeth. He said they got fed three times a day with raw meat and were very intelligent and clever, and if they would wait a minute he would run and fetch some meat and show them how they did their tricks.

He went off, and while he was gone Mary chatted to Elisabeth. At least, it wasn't quite chatting, because Elisabeth wouldn't answer. Mary asked her five times, each time a little louder, whether she liked being called Elisabeth, and she just took no notice at all.

'She must be deaf too,' said Mary, giving it up, and just then the keeper came back.

'If you will step up here,' he said, 'you'll get a better view.' And they went up some steps and on to a tiny platform, and the man had to lock the gate behind them, because lots of little boys tried to come on to it too. 'Get off! You know you're not allowed here,' he said roughly.

'Only us,' said Mary, from the right side of the railings.

'Now, come on Babs,' shouted the keeper, and he threw a large bit of raw meat into the water, and Babs dived in – a graceful, 'leaving-one-foot-behind' kind of dive – and before the meat had reached the bottom she had caught it. Then the man shouted, 'Now, Sam!' Sam stood up and saluted.

'And how about Elisabeth?' asked the Owl Man, and the keeper laughed and said he was afraid Elisabeth was a slow old thing and not up to doing tricks.

Next they visited the seals. One large black fellow was asleep on a rock, looking like a huge handbag stuffed full of things. But his wife, who was brown, was not sleepy, and she began making hungry noises close beside him and woke him up. He had long black whiskers, and he started honking like a car horn, and they made a fearsome duet. So Mary and the Owl Man crossed over to the ostrich, who lived just opposite. It had its head buried in the sandy pebbles and looked very foolish.

'What is it doing?' asked Mary.

'Hiding,' said the Owl Man.

'But it's still there.'

'Yes, I know, but ostriches are always like that; when they hide their heads they think the rest of them is hidden too.'

'Shall I tell him he isn't?' asked Mary.

'I don't think I should bother,' said the Owl Man.

Next came the Lion House, and it was feeding time, and everyone who has been in the Lion House at feeding time knows what that means.

But Mary did not know, and she held the Owl Man's hand very tight, and was glad of the bars.

Next they visited Simba.

Simba had just been fed, and looked the picture of a very fine and extremely full lion. He was lying by the bars and licking his lips. There was a keeper near by, and as the Owl Man went over to talk to him, Mary asked if she might go and have a little chat with Simba.

'Certainly,' said the Owl Man. 'But mind you don't get into any trouble, Mary Plain.'

Mary approached the huge lion quite timidly, for the lion is the king of all beasts.

'Good morning, Sir,' she said respectfully.

Simba turned his head slowly. 'Good morning,' he said, 'who are you?'

'I am Mary Plain, an unusual first prize Swiss bear from the pits at Berne, and I am nearly one,' said Mary, and hoped she had impressed His Majesty.

'You seem to be a good many things,' said Simba good-humouredly.

'Yes,' said Mary, 'I have been unusual for a long time, but I have only been first class since yesterday – at the Show.' She hoped very much that Simba would ask her about the Show, so she could tell him she had won a rosette, but Simba, it seemed, was not interested in shows.

'I have travelled a lot too,' said Mary, 'in a tram, and a car, and a train, and a ship and – and – a net.'

Simba's ears cocked slowly. Everything he did was slow and majestic.

'I have travelled too,' he said.

'Oh, do tell me,' begged Mary.

'Well it was a long while ago now,' said Simba. 'I belonged to a kind lady who brought me in a big ship to this country – England, I think it is called –'

'English spoken,' said Mary, who was in a very showing-off mood.

Simba, however, did not speak English, and only said, 'I would rather you did not interrupt me, please.' Mary stopped feeling showy-off and felt a very small bear indeed.

'I lived in a garden for a bit,' went on Simba, 'and then, one day, the lady brought me here, and here I have been ever since,' he finished sadly. 'For though she came to see me at first, she has not been for a long time now, and I think she has forgotten me.'

Mary felt suddenly sick. The lady had brought Simba here – the Owl Man had brought her here, and he was talking to the keeper too. She sidled up to him and jerked his arm. The Owl Man looked down and saw that she was trembling.

'Mary,' he said, 'whatever is the matter?'

'I don't think the twins are happy without me,' she said in a wobbly voice, 'and I want to go home at once – now, please, this very minute!'

The Owl Man looked very astonished and said she really must tell him why she felt like that.

'Simba,' said Mary with a gulp. 'He came with his kind lady, and she left him behind all alone, and he's been in that enclosure ever since.'

The Owl Man saw at once what Mary was afraid of.

'Perhaps,' he said, 'but Simba wasn't just a visitor, was he? You run across and ask him.' So Mary went back to Simba.

'Were you a svisitor?' she asked.

'What is that?' asked Simba in a surprised voice.

'It's what you are on a svisit – a stop or a – or a go-to,' explained Mary.

'No,' said Simba, 'I've always been a lion.'

Mary heaved a sigh of relief, and at that moment the Owl Man came up.

'Well, Mary Plain,' he said kindly, 'feeling happy again? I know just exactly what you were thinking of, you know.'

'But you wouldn't, would you?' said Mary.

'Definitely not,' said the Owl Man. 'Let's go and see the elephants.'

On their way they passed the ostrich, still with its head sticking into the pebbles. Mary felt sorrier than ever about it. Then they went down under a bridge and up the other side, and there were the elephants.

Each elephant had its name written up over it, and the Owl Man read them out: Ranee and Heera Cully. Heera Cully shot out his long trunk and blew at Mary, and she backed away.

'What is that he's blowing at me with?' she asked.

The Owl Man told her it was his trunk, and how it was like an extra paw to an elephant, and how he lifted his food up to his mouth with it.

'He wouldn't lift me, would he?' said Mary anxiously.

'Not he. You give him this bun and see him eat it.'

Then Mary made a very long arm so as not to be too near and gave Heera Cully a bun, and he twisted up his trunk and popped it into his mouth, and it was very funny.

But all the time they were seeing the elephants, Mary was worrying about the ostrich. It did seem so sad he should think he was hidden when all the time he was there. If only someone would tell him about it he could be more careful.

The Owl Man began chatting to the attendant, and Mary edged nearer and nearer to the door, and the next minute she was galloping down the wide path that goes under the bridge on her way back to the ostrich.

But somehow she must have taken the wrong turning for when she got to the place where she was sure the ostrich was, there was only a buffalo.

'Could you tell me where the ostrich lives?' she asked in a panty voice, for she was quite out of breath.

'What does it look like?' said the buffalo.

'Well, it's made of heaps of curly feathers, and it's fond of hide-and-seek,' said Mary. The buffalo shook his head.

'There's a wolf over there who is particularly fond of cheese,' he said, but that was no help at all, so Mary set off on her hunt again.

How it happened it is difficult to know, but one small boy saw Mary and gave the alarm, 'A little bear has got loose.' And from all directions people came running towards Mary shouting, 'Send for the keeper – try and stop it – catch it – hasn't anyone got a rope?'

Mary took fright and made off round a corner, and the faster she ran the faster the people ran after her.

158

And the crowd got bigger and bigger, and half the people ran because the other people were running and had no idea what they were running after.

'What is it?' gasped one pursuer, and another shouted, 'A little bear has got loose,' and then another said, 'A big bear has got loose,' and then it changed to 'A dangerous bear has got loose,' and by the time Mary swung round a corner by the sea-lion pond a hundred-and-fifty people were all screaming, 'Beware of the man-eating bear!'

By this time Mary was thoroughly frightened, and when she saw a keeper with a rope in his hand trying to cut her off from the side, she made a final dash for safety and swarmed up a telegraph pole.

There she sat in perfect security and looked down at her chasers, all clamouring at the bottom of the pole.

'If only you'd been a bit more nippy with that rope, Jack,' said one keeper.

'Nippy yourself,' said Jack crossly. He had run half a mile as fast as he could after Mary, and it was a hot day.

'She'll never come down now,' said another keeper, called Fred, 'she's taken fright.'

'Till she's hungry,' added Jack. And he was quite right.

Sitting up there Mary was safe; but she was also empty, and though, when you have been chased, safety is a delicious feeling – emptiness is not.

Mary began to wriggle. She longed for the Owl Man and searched for a kind face among the crowd below.

Picking out a young man with a freckled nose who was standing close to the pole, she said, with a choke, 'Do you think the twins are happy without me?' But the man was no Swiss scholar, so he couldn't answer.

'What would you do if she came down?' asked Jack.

'Take her to the Lost Property Office. She doesn't belong to us; that's all we could do,' said Fred.

Mary stared round miserably. 'Could somebody fetch the Owl Man?' she pleaded, but nobody understood, so Mary hung on to the pole and went on being hungry.

'Tell you what, Jack,' said Fred, 'let's get all this crowd away and then put a plate of meat down at the bottom. I bet she'd come down after it and then we could rope her in a jiffy.'

And Fred was right. When the crowd had been sent away they put a tempting dish just at the foot of the pole, and Mary sniffed and came, very nervously, a little way down. Then she took fright and scrambled up again, but soon the smell was too strong for her, and she slid down; this time nearer to the ground, and that meant nearer to the smell, and when she actually saw the lovely bits of meat with tips of carrots among it, she gave up all idea of 'Safety first', and slid the rest of the way down.

Almost before she touched the earth she was neatly lassoed, and within a few minutes she was standing among a lot of umbrellas and handbags in the Lost Property Office, while several hot keepers stood near by and mopped their faces.

They had been very kind and given her the meat to eat as soon as she was safely in the Lost Property Office, and Mary tucked into it busily.

Suddenly there came the sound of running footsteps, and one of the keepers went to the door. 'Someone in a hurry,' he said.

Outside was the poor Owl Man, so red in the face that the keeper felt sorry for him. 'Lost something, sir?' he asked kindly. 'A bear,' gasped the Owl Man. 'A small bear. Seen her anywhere?'

'Yes, he has, I'm here,' yelled Mary from among the umbrellas.

So the Owl Man went in, and they brought him a chair to sit on, and he sat and patted Mary and panted, and it was a little time before he could speak again.

Then Mary told him all about what had happened, and the Owl Man said that ended it once for all; she should wear her collar and lead till they got back to Berne.

'But I felt so sorry about the ostrich,' protested Mary.

'I'm the person you ought to feel sorry about,' said the still-out-of-breath Owl Man, and he looked so red that Mary really did pity him.

When he had cooled off, and had a drink they went and found the car and drove home, and Mary was very quiet on the way. This was so unusual that the Owl Man asked her what she was thinking about.

'I'm thinking I'm very glad I haven't got a luggage like that elephant,' said Mary. 'I like paws best.'

Chapter Fourteen

How Berne welcomed Mary home

Mary set to work very seriously over her packing next morning, but even she couldn't take very long over one brush and one bowl, so she wandered in to help the Owl Man do his. But after she had packed a bottle of shampoo among his shirts without the top on, the Owl Man said he thought perhaps he'd better do his own packing, and she could sit and talk to him while he did it.

So he put Mary on top of a chest of drawers safely out of the way, and she drummed her paws on the chest and decided, very kindly, to sing him a song, so he shouldn't be bored.

'I shall sing you a song,' she announced.

'That will be delightful,' said the Owl Man.

'It's a song about bears,' said Mary.

'No, really?' said the Owl Man. Mary nodded.

'And it's *very* exciting,' she said.

'As long as it doesn't distract me from my packing,' said the Owl Man.

'Now,' said Mary, and began.

But first she began too high and then she began too low, and then it took her some time to find the note she wanted in-between. But once she found it she wasn't going to risk losing it again, so she sang all the song on it, and this was the song she sang:

> *'Once there was a bear called Alpha.*
> *Once there was a bear called Lady Grizzle.*
> *Once there was a bear called Harrods.*
> *Once there was a bear called Bunch.*
> *Once there was a bear called Big Wool.*
> *Once there was a bear called Friska.*
> *Once there was a bear called Little Wool.*
> *Once there was a bear called Marionetta.'*

Here she broke off for a second because she wanted

to ask the Owl Man a question; but because of her fear of losing the note she sang it at him all on the same note.

'Aren't you getting very excited?' she sang.
'Ter – ri – bly,' sang back the Owl Man.
'There's only the last verse left,' sang Mary.
'And once there was a bear called MARY PLAIN.'
'A – men,' chanted the Owl Man.

'What men?' said Mary, looking round.

'Nothing,' said the Owl Man, 'No men at all. I like your song immensely, Mary Plain.'

'Shall I sing it again?'

'Well, perhaps another time,' said the Owl Man hurriedly. 'I tell you what, I've never shown you your presents to take back to the other bears, have I?'

'Me? Presents? Mine?' said Mary, and in her excitement she fell off the chest with a whack.

The Owl Man picked her up and took her into a room where there were eight brightly-coloured bowls all standing in a row on the floor.

They were really the loveliest bowls, and Mary danced up and down when she saw them. Every bowl had its name on it, beginning with Big Wool on the biggest and so on down to the two smallest. Mary examined each one and the Owl Man read her out the names. When she got to the small ones, she said, 'But who are these for?'

'For the aunts,' said the Owl Man.

'And what are their names?' inquired Mary.

'Forget-me-not and Plum,' said the Owl Man.

'I don't think Get-me-not's a nice name,' said Mary.

'For-get-me-not,' corrected the Owl Man.

'Yes, I know it's for Get-me-not, but I don't think it's a nice name,' persisted Mary.

'But her name is *Forget*-me-not,' said the Owl Man.

'Who has she forgotten, and why has she got three names?' said Mary, in a jealous voice, but the Owl Man really didn't know, and left Mary to gaze at the bowls while he finished his own packing.

'You know, we are flying today,' said the Owl Man, as they were eating their lunch.

'On Robin?' asked Mary, remembering a dream she had once had.

'No, in an aeroplane,' said the Owl Man; 'it will be a case of "Mary Plain, in an aeroplane," won't it?' but he was sorry he had been funny, because Mary was so amused that she swallowed a potato the wrong way and had to be shaken by the heels to get it back.

They drove down to the place they were to fly from, which was like a big flat field, and in the middle was a huge bird with silver wings, and it was the aeroplane.

The pilot was standing talking to some of the passengers, but as soon as he saw Mary he came over and spoke to her.

'Are you one of my passengers?' he asked.

'No,' said Mary, 'I am Mary Plain.'

'But you are one of his passengers, too, Mary,' said the Owl Man.

'That's great,' said the pilot. 'Do you know, I believe this is the first time I've ever had the pleasure of piloting a bear.'

'Is it a pleasure?' asked Mary.

'A very great one, I assure you,' said the pilot.

'But I have flown before,' said Mary.

'Have you indeed?'

'Yes, once in a dream and once in a net,' said Mary, and she told him about how she had got mixed up with the mail.

Mary had no flying clothes, so the pilot very kindly lent her a helmet, and when she had put it on it was time to start. Mary's short legs were a little inconvenient for getting into the plane, so she had to be lifted, and when she got inside there were little seats down the sides, and hers was the front seat of all.

A man came round and gave them paper bags, and Mary thought him very kind till she found the bags were empty.

'The biscuits have all gone,' she complained to the Owl Man, who was sitting just behind her. It was a bit awkward for him, because he did not want to tell her that the bag was in case she felt sick, for fear it should put it into her mind to *be* sick, so he said, 'I think he just wants us to take care of it for him on the journey. Tuck it into the corner of your seat so it will be safe.'

As soon as the engines started Mary decided she would walk home. She had to climb down off her seat and go and shout in the Owl Man's ear to be heard above the noise.

'Nonsense!' he said, 'flying is the greatest fun,' and he lifted her straight back to her seat. He felt a firm hand was the only hope, because a 'Mary' scene in an aeroplane would be too much to bear.

up and away!
AIR
Miss Mary Plain

Mary promptly got down again and came and shouted that she didn't think they were very friendly chairs with all their backs turned and only an empty bag beside you. The Owl Man was just going to be firm again, when Mary said, 'Do you think the twins are happy without me?' so, instead, he said if she was very good she could sit on his little case by his feet, and Mary sat down and held his ankle for company and was much happier.

Now, however comforting a grey silk ankle may be, it isn't exactly exciting, so when Mary felt a tap on her shoulder and understood by the Owl Man's pointings that if she was on her chair she could see better, she nodded her head and consented to be put back again. Then she looked out, and there was the earth, so tiny that it didn't look like the earth at all, and while Mary was looking it all got blue underneath and it was the sea.

When they had flown over some more land, they began to go round and round and down and down, a little bit like when the lift went down, but not so bad, and then they could see little black dots moving below, and soon they were low enough to see they were people, and they had arrived.

'I like aeroplaning better than netting,' said Mary, as she said goodbye to the pilot.

'That's splendid,' he said, as he shook her paw.

'Yes, I liked it all, except the empty bags,' said Mary.

'Empty bags?' said the pilot, looking bewildered.

So the Owl Man explained about Mary's appetite and how it never got tired, and the pilot said, 'One moment please,' and ran off.

In a minute he came back with two bulging paper bags, one full of biscuits and the other with bananas and peaches in it.

'Thank you,' Mary said, 'bags look nicer fat than flat, don't they?'

'How soon before they are flat again?' murmured the Owl Man, but Mary was too engaged with a peach to answer.

The rest of the journey went very smoothly. Mary was drowsy after the flying and slept soundly all night, and when they woke up there was only just time for a hurried breakfast before they were at Berne.

Mary began to feel very excited.

The Owl Man's feelings were mixed. He was sorry to part with Mary, but, on the other hand, he couldn't help feeling relieved that he had got her back safely. Travelling with Mary was anxious work, and now that was all over; they only had to go a short taxi ride and Mary would be back in her pit and all his responsibility at an end.

But alas, for once the Owl Man was forgetting that Mary was an unusual bear – and not only that, but since she had been to the Earl's Court Show and won first prize, she was also a famous bear!

The people of Berne, however, had not forgotten, and nearly all of them had come to meet Mary at the station.

When the train began to slow down the Owl Man went into the corridor to call a porter, and he saw, to his astonishment, that the whole station was one mass of bobbing heads and waving flags. Just opposite their carriage was a group of officials and behind them a band.

'Whatever's happened?' the Owl Man asked the man nearest to the door. 'Is somebody important arriving or something?'

'Yes,' said the man, 'the famous bear is returning by this train, and the Mayor and Town Council have all come to welcome her home.'

'Great heavens above!' said the Owl Man distractedly, and rushed back to collect Mary.

There was no escape. The Owl Man ground his teeth. Of all the things that Mary had done to him this was by far the worst. But though he might wish himself in Timbuctoo, it didn't help at all, because here he was in Berne, and outside were all the inhabitants of Berne waiting for Mary.

'Now, Mary, listen carefully,' he said in a hurried whisper, and as he spoke he slipped her rosette round her neck. 'There are a lot of people outside – they have come to welcome you home, and with them are the Mayor and Town Council.'

'And what are they?' said Mary.

'Very important persons indeed, Mary,' said the Owl Man, 'and you must be as polite as you know how. Their coming to meet you like this is a very great honour.'

'On who?' asked Mary, as the Owl Man hurried her along to the door. Luckily the loud cheer that greeted her as she appeared in the doorway drove all other thoughts out of Mary's mind.

As she stepped onto the platform, holding very tightly to the Owl Man's hand, a roll on the drums and cries of 'Welcome home! Well done, Mary Plain! – Your country is proud of you – Long live Mary Plain!' went echoing round the station.

It was an alarming ordeal for a small bear to face, even when the bear was as well-travelled as Mary.

The Mayor was a plump man with a booming voice. He bowed low over Mary's paw, and he stayed so long bowing that she patted him kindly on the head with the other paw. Then she shook hands with all the Town Council, and then the Mayor cleared his throat and someone cried, 'Silence for His Honour the Mayor.'

The Mayor went on clearing his throat till everyone was quite silent, and then Mary asked him anxiously if he thought he had caught a cold.

'Ssh, Mary,' said the Owl Man, 'don't speak – listen.' And the Mayor read:

'We, the Mayor and Town Council, together with these loyal citizens of Berne, have one and all gathered here to welcome you home, Mary Plain, and to tell you that we are proud that you should have brought such fame to your home town.'

'I haven't got any fame, but I've got some bowls for

the bears,' said Mary.

'Will you be quiet, Mary!' said the Owl Man from behind.

'I feel', boomed the Mayor, 'that it is an immense pleasure and privilege that, as Mayor of this said city of Berne, it should fall to me to offer you our most sincere congratulations and to lead this great and, may I say, enthusiastic welcome.'

Here he had to break off because the cheers broke out afresh, and Mary tugged at the Owl Man's hand and whispered, 'I'm tired of this man.'

'Hush, Mary, for heaven's sake!' said the Owl Man.

The Mayor made a large gesture with his hand. 'I think these honest people's voices tell you better than I can how proud we feel of you, and I will now, in the name of the city of Berne, present you with this medal.'

Here the Mayor stepped forward and slipped a gilt chain round Mary's neck and on the end of it was a big flat medal, like a gold penny. Mary examined it. 'Why,' she exclaimed, 'it's a picture of me, all in gold!' And everyone cheered some more, and just then a procession approached.

174

It was all the pastry cooks of Berne, and each one had tried to see if he couldn't make the best cake, and all the cakes were for Mary. The most exciting of all was a chocolate bear cake.

Then the Mayor said, if Mary would step forward, a car was all ready waiting to take her to the pits; but just at that moment Mary caught sight of the Fancy-Coat-Lady who had come to meet her too, and she was thrilled.

'Hooray, and how-do-you-do, Fancy-Coat-Lady!' she shouted. 'You must come here and help me choose which is the nicest cake.'

'But you can't possibly start choosing now, Mary,' said the Owl Man in despair. He knew how long Mary's cake decisions took.

'I won't move till I have some of that chocolate bear,' said Mary. Her legs began to brace, so the Owl Man knew she meant it; they quickly chopped off some of the bear, and Mary, with her mouth quite full of head and her paw full of hind leg, consented to follow the Mayor.

It was not an ordinary kind of car, but a lorry, and in it they had built a platform, all decorated with flowers, for Mary to stand on.

When Mary appeared she was, for the first time,

in full view of everyone, and they began shouting and calling, 'Speech! Speech!'

'I'm very sorry,' Mary shouted, 'but I ate the last one for my breakfast this morning.'

'No, no, Mary,' said the Owl Man. '"Speech" means that they want you to say a few words.'

'Oh, words,' said Mary, 'I see.' She thought for a moment and then she said, very loud, 'Svisits – meringues – rosettes – netting – cream buns – bathing costume –' before they managed to stop her. Then they did some whispering. Mary nodded and started again.

'All of you,' she said, 'I am glad you are glad about me. Thank you,' and she bowed deeply, and the Owl Man said she couldn't have done it better.

Then the procession started for the pits.

First the band, playing a welcoming march, then the Mayor and Town Council, and then Mary in her lorry. And all the people shouted and sang, and all the little boys threw their hats into the air, and flags were waved out of the windows, and Mary bowed and waved and saluted all the way.

When they reached the pits, Mary insisted on the lorry being driven close to the edge so the other bears could see her. When the bears heard the band

and looked up – there was Mary, standing on the platform in all her glory, taller than anyone else.

'God save the Queen,' said Mary, saluting.

Big Wool saluted back, and Friska lost her head completely and curtsied to the ground, and even Bunch clapped with stiff paws, and as for the twins – well, they nearly burst with excitement.

And then all the Town Council and the Mayor had to be said 'Goodbye' to, and last of all the Fancy-Coat-Lady and the Owl Man.

They stood by the entrance to Nursery Pit, and the Owl Man patted Mary on the head.

'Well, Mary Plain,' he said, 'I am glad to have got you safely back, and I am sad to say goodbye,' and he really did look it.

Mary stared up at him, and then she turned and looked through the railings.

'Twins,' she shouted, 'were you happy without me?'

'NO!' roared the twins.

Mary turned back. 'So you see,' she said, 'I have to go back.'

'Yes, that settles it,' said the Owl Man. 'Well, goodbye, Mary Plain, we shall meet again soon, and in the meantime you'd better have a good sleep – you must be tired out.'

She was indeed; but a good sleep soon put her right again and made her feel as fresh as anything for the party she gave that night.

There were all the bears and all the lovely cakes at the beginning of the party, but at the end there were only the bears.

Then Mary presented the bowls, and they were all very proud and pleased, and Big Wool said, 'Three cheers for Mary', and they gave her a bear cheer.

And all the people of Berne on their way home to bed stopped and wondered as they heard, far away, 'Hip, hip, hoo-Mary – Hip, hip, hoo-Plain.'

THE ADVENTURES OF
Mary Plain

Get ready to welcome back beloved bear
Mary Plain in this exciting relaunch of
Gwynedd Rae's much-loved classic series.

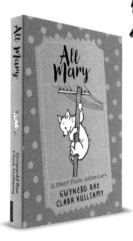

Brand new illustrations by Clara Vulliamy
will introduce Mary Plain and friends to
a whole new generation of readers.

Look out for *Mary Plain in Town* and
Mary Plain in America coming soon.